"Hey, Seth! Did you corral that filly?"

"Got her right here." Seth slapped the side of the car and grinned.

Claire stayed put. "I am not a horse." No one heard her.

"I'll admit I'm surprised, Seth. New Yorkers can be mighty stubborn."

"I am not a horse," Claire repeated. "And I do not wish to be referred to as one."

Seth finally noticed that she wasn't getting out of the car. "Did you say something?"

"I *said* I am not a horse!"

Seth blinked. The afternoon sun shone in his face, and his eyelashes cast shadows on his cheeks. "Ma'am—Claire—no one has called you a horse."

"*He*—" she pointed "—said filly."

"Well, yes, ma'am, I suppose he did, but he didn't mean to be disrespectful."

Privately, Claire thought that was exactly what the old rancher had meant, but she had made her point. Accepting the hand Seth offered, she exited the car as gracefully as she could.

Dear Reader,

Harlequin Romance would like to welcome you back to the ranch again with our yearlong miniseries, **HITCHED!** We've rounded up twelve of our most popular authors, and the result is a whole year of romance Western style: cool cowboys, rugged ranchers and, of course, the women who tame them.

Next month it's the turn of Catherine Leigh and *Something Old, Something New*. Lily Alexander's husband, Saige, had been missing—presumed dead—for seven long years when he walked back into her life! And though Lily's heart rejoiced at his return, the timing was awkward, to say the least. Lily's wedding to her new fiancé was imminent. But how could Lily marry placid lawyer Randall when her sexy rancher husband refused to let her go?

Look out for books branded **HITCHED!** in the coming months.

Happy reading, partners!

The Editors,
Harlequin Romance

How the West was wooed!

Temporary Texan

Heather Allison

Harlequin Books

TORONTO • NEW YORK • LONDON
AMSTERDAM • PARIS • SYDNEY • HAMBURG
STOCKHOLM • ATHENS • TOKYO • MILAN
MADRID • WARSAW • BUDAPEST • AUCKLAND

If you purchased this book without a cover you should be aware that this book is stolen property. It was reported as "unsold and destroyed" to the publisher, and neither the author nor the publisher has received any payment for this "stripped book."

ISBN 0-373-03421-0

TEMPORARY TEXAN

First North American Publication 1996.

Copyright © 1996 by Heather W. MacAllister.

All rights reserved. Except for use in any review, the reproduction or utilization of this work in whole or in part in any form by any electronic, mechanical or other means, now known or hereafter invented, including xerography, photocopying and recording, or in any information storage or retrieval system, is forbidden without the written permission of the publisher, Harlequin Enterprises Limited, 225 Duncan Mill Road, Don Mills, Ontario, Canada M3B 3K9.

All characters in this book have no existence outside the imagination of the author and have no relation whatsoever to anyone bearing the same name or names. They are not even distantly inspired by any individual known or unknown to the author, and all incidents are pure invention.

This edition published by arrangement with Harlequin Books S.A.

® and TM are trademarks of the publisher. Trademarks indicated with ® are registered in the United States Patent and Trademark Office, the Canadian Trade Marks Office and in other countries.

Printed in U.S.A.

CHAPTER ONE

"WHAT do you think of my latest designs? Are they good enough to win the scholarship to study in Paris?" For the past ten minutes, Claire Bellingham had waited impatiently while Audrey, of Audrey's Boutique in Greenwich Village, New York, flipped through the sketchbook.

"Mmm," Audrey said, paging through the sketches again.

"Oh, great!" Claire threw up her arms and paced from the markdown rack to the stairs leading to the loft. "My entry has to go in the mail this afternoon and all I get is 'mmm.'"

"The designs are good. You know they are, but I was trying to view them as if I were seeing them for the first time." Audrey looked over her half glasses at Claire. "Instead of having sold several of these in the shop already."

"Sorry," Claire mumbled. A flash from the display window caught her eye, and she wandered over. The sun reflected off a pair of earrings dangling from a wire mannequin form. "Hey, I don't remember these earrings."

"We got them in yesterday. I unpacked last night."

"Oh." There was no censure in Audrey's voice, even though Claire normally would have stayed after the shop closed to help unpack the latest shipment. After all, it was her job. But she'd been working on the last of the design sketches to enter in the Fashion Academy of Paris's annual contest. She'd entered every year because she was determined to study fashion design from a Paris master. And that was the top prize—a full scholarship to the academy and apprenticeship in a designer's atelier. Each year of the four years she'd worked in Audrey's Boutique, Claire had sketched and resketched until the last minute. And Audrey had always indulged her.

But Audrey had never studied her book this long before, either. A nervous Claire fingered the earrings on the mannequin. "Austrian crystal?"

"Yes," Audrey confirmed, still studying the drawings.

The earrings sparkled again, luring Claire closer. She just happened to be wearing a purple suede miniskirt with a pink mohair sweater. And these earrings just happened to be pink, white and purple. Audrey had draped a chiffon scarf swirling with just those shades around the mannequin's neck.

Perfect. Claire had accessorized her outfit in silver. This morning, she'd liked the contrast of the hard cold metal against the fluffy girlish sweater. Now, she changed her mind. Whipping off her silver belt, she tied the scarf around her waist and exchanged her long obelisk earrings for the glittering crystal ones.

But now the display was all wrong. Claire could wear a scarf around her waist, but the mannequin couldn't wear a belt around her neck. That would be...

Brilliant! "Audrey! I need some paper!"

Audrey thumbed through to the back of the book she held and prepared to rip out a sheet.

"Not from there!" Claire protested. "The edges will show." She fumbled behind the counter, grabbing a paper sack when nothing else came to hand. Quickly, she drew a picture of her latest brainstorm.

She was barely aware of Audrey coming to stand and watch her. Within moments, Claire held up the sack. "There!" She turned it so Audrey could see. "Should I substitute this dress for one of the designs in the book?"

"Belts?" Audrey glanced from the sack to Claire. "A woman wearing just belts?"

"No, see . . . a narrow belt around her neck, a wider one across the bust and the widest around the hips, all connected with transparent tissue faille." Claire set the design on the counter and drew legs, then a belt around one thigh as a garter. "What do you think? Leather for daytime, rhinestone buckles for evening?"

Audrey crossed her arms and eyed Claire. "I can see that this design would appeal to a certain type of woman. We don't get too many of them in here."

Claire frowned. "The transparent panels are too much?"

"Are you asking my opinion?" Audrey gave her a stern look. "Because you shouldn't have to. It's your design. Only you should say whether see-through is too much. You should *know*. You should have vision."

Claire crumpled the sack with the buckle dress design and tossed it at the rattan wastebasket. She missed. "I don't have a vision. That's why I need to go to Paris."

Uncrossing her arms, Audrey nodded and picked up Claire's book. "These are good," she said again. "But they're all so different."

"Of course," Claire said with surprise. "This year I'm showing my versatility."

"But you aren't showing your style."

Claire hadn't settled on a personal signature style. Each season, she tried something different. "The last three years, the judges haven't liked the style I've shown them. This year, I'm hoping at least *one* of these looks appeals to *somebody.*"

With a deep breath, she closed the sketchbook and slipped it into the already addressed envelope. She was determined to study in Paris and soon. If she didn't win a scholarship this year, she'd scrape together the money and go anyway. It wouldn't be easy, but she'd do it. She had to.

"I'm on my way to the post office," she said, waving goodbye to Audrey.

"Good luck!"

I feel lucky, Claire thought, stepping onto the sidewalk and heading toward the post office.

As she walked along the Greenwich Village streets and tried to ignore the stench from the blooming ginkgo trees, Claire automatically studied the women around her, analyzing what they were wearing this spring. Of course she was already thinking fall and the holidays, but some trends spanned seasons.

She reached the post office without seeing anything new, just noting that jeans and boots were everywhere. Jeans and boots, jeans and boots. She'd never worked in denim. Perhaps she should. Reaching the window, she crossed her fingers, then watched as the postal clerk stamped the padded envelope containing her contest entry.

And that was that.

Claire exhaled and felt the energy drain out of her. She'd spent every spare minute working this past week. Now it was time for life to get back to normal. Yawning, she walked around the bank of post office boxes looking for her own. She hadn't checked her mail for an entire week. Not that she ever got much mail.

This time, though, her box was full. Sorting through the letters, Claire wandered over to the trash can and tossed in her junk mail without opening it.

Three credit card applications—they obviously were taking anybody these days—a coupon book and a record club pitch all ended up in the trash. Two small yellow notices fluttered in after them. Claire fished them out of the bin. Two registered letters. Nuts. She'd have to sign for them, which meant another wait in line.

As the post office line inched forward, Claire nervously tried to guess who had sent her what. It was awful news, this she knew. Good news arrived with flowers. Bad news required a lengthy wait in a post office line.

At last, a clerk handed her two overnight letter packets. Each contained a stark-white envelope with the return address of a law firm engraved in the corner.

Lawyers plus registered letters equaled trouble. Heart accelerating, Claire opened the one bearing the oldest postmark first and began scanning the letter before it was completely unfolded.

"We regret to inform you of the death of your grandfather, John Beauregard Bellingham, on April 18." Claire looked up from her letter. Over a week ago. And she hadn't known. Her eyes burned with the incipient tears of regret and grief. And guilt. She and her grandfather weren't particularly close, but he had kept in touch with Claire. Unlike his son, her father, whom she hadn't seen or heard from once her parents divorced.

Why hadn't someone *called* her? Didn't they think she'd want to know? Why hadn't her mother called her? Granted, Claire's mother hadn't been Beau Bellingham's daughter-in-law for over fifteen years, but surely she'd been notified of Beau's death. Or perhaps not. Claire's family didn't keep tabs on each other.

The rest of the letter informed Claire that funeral arrangements were pending.

Slowly, she tore open the second envelope, dreading its contents. As she suspected, she'd missed the funeral. It would have meant dipping into her Paris fund to fly to Texas for it, but Claire would have.

Without bothering to sort through the rest of her mail, Claire numbly walked to Audrey's. She was sad but not grief-stricken. The last time she'd seen her grandfather had been at her college graduation six years earlier. And the time before that had been at her high school graduation. And the time before that...

The summer her parents divorced. Claire had spent the entire summer with her grandfather at Bellingham Ranch. Her constantly fighting and bickering parents had looked on it as a kind of summer camp—except much cheaper.

Claire hadn't minded. It had been a relief to get away from the quarrels. She'd been thirteen and horse mad, but by August, she hadn't cared if she saw another horse for as long as she lived.

Ranching was hard work, and Claire's fantasies of spending the day on horseback exploring the world had ended with her first case of saddle soreness.

Horses also required a lot of upkeep. That's when Claire discovered her allergy to hay and grass, dust and animal dander.

No, ranching wasn't for her, but she'd always remembered Beau with fondness. They wrote each other on birthdays and Christmas and pretended that Claire would come back for another summer. She never had.

And now her grandfather was gone.

The only way to find out what had happened would be to contact the law firm, which Claire decided she'd do this afternoon during her break. Arriving at the boutique and pushing open the side door, she vowed to call her mother, too.

"I'm back," Claire called to let Audrey know who was in the workroom. After quickly running a brush through her short dark hair, Claire reapplied her scarlet lipstick then locked her purse in the desk. Black hair, white skin, red lips—that was her trademark look. When was anyone going to notice?

"Claire." Audrey pushed aside the beaded curtain separating the boutique from the workroom and beckoned to her. "Someone would like to speak with you."

What now? Claire wondered, unable to read anything in Audrey's blank expression.

As soon as she stepped into the salesroom, Claire's eyes were drawn to the sable-haired man staring out the display window. She had no idea who he was, but good heavens, he was tall. Claire doubted she even reached his shoulders, impressively broad shoulders, she noted, with both a tailor's eye and a feminine one.

He turned when he heard their footsteps, and Claire saw that though he was dressed in a dark, well-cut business suit, he held a cowboy hat in his hands. She checked, and sure enough, he wore boots. Claire had seen this look before, especially when the Western craze swept Manhattan a few seasons ago. But this man wasn't making a fashion statement—he was living one.

Audrey urged her forward. "Mr. Montgomery, this is Claire Bellingham."

"Thank you, ma'am."

Claire's gaze shot from the man's boots to his tanned face as his surprisingly deep voice drawled toward her, twanging something inside her. Smiling perfunctorily, he nodded to Audrey, who discreetly moved to the other side of the shop.

Claire had already extended her hand for him to shake when he turned hard brown eyes toward her. For the briefest instant, she thought he wasn't going to shake her hand, and it took her aback.

But he did shake her hand, gripping it with a pressure just short of painful. It was a man-to-man grip, not a man-to-woman grip. Normally, Claire appreciated a firm grip, but she'd been feverishly drawing the past several days and her hands already ached. Nevertheless, she felt it was important to hold on and match squeeze for squeeze, as if this was a test instead of a handshake.

"Miss Bellingham."

Claire received a nod similar to Audrey's, but without the smile. What a shame. A smile would have softened the hard line of his jaw. He did smile on occasion. Now that she was closer to him, she could see the squint lines around his eyes.

"Mr. Montgomery."

He was handsome, but a grump. She waited for him to state his business, or at least let her know why he seemed to be angry.

He remained silent, looking at her. Claire saw his eyes flick over her, lingering on her feet. She wished her sweater wasn't quite so tight, her suede skirt wasn't quite so mini and her boots weren't quite so... silver.

She also wished he'd say something. "You wanted to see me?" she prompted, irritated at his increasingly obvious contempt.

He drew a sharp breath and began speaking, the drawl not nearly as pronounced. "I'm Seth Montgomery," he stated as though the name would mean something to her.

It didn't. "Claire Bellingham." Claire restrained herself from offering her hand again.

His brow wrinkled. "You don't know who I am?"

"Should I?" Claire was in no mood to play guessing games. "Did somebody set us up on a blind date and forget to tell me?"

The corner of his mouth lifted. It might have been the beginnings of a smile, but Claire suspected it was a sneer.

"I'm the president of CENTOR, the Central Texas Ostrich Ranchers." He continued when it was obvious Claire had no idea what he was talking about. "We're a coalition of ranchers who've pooled our resources to raise ostriches."

Claire still had no clue why he was in Audrey's shop talking about ostriches. "I'm afraid I don't..."

"Ma'am, are you Beau Bellingham's granddaughter?"

Claire, still absorbing the news that her grandfather had died, could only nod.

"I see." After a moment, Mr. Montgomery shifted his hat from one hand to the other and took her elbow. "May we sit over there?" He indicated the ornate wooden high-backed chairs on either side of the dressing room door.

Claire felt a feminine flutter as the tall rancher—did he say his name was Seth?—guided her through the boutique. She'd never gone for the sturdy outdoors type, and taking in his tanned face and hands, she surmised that Seth was definitely an outdoors type. How interesting to discover that she was as susceptible to a manly man as the next woman. She'd file that away for future reference.

He waited until she was seated before he pulled the other chair closer to her and sat. Leaning forward, his expression gentle, he spoke. "Miss Bellingham—"

"Do call me Claire. You're making me nervous."

He blinked twice. "I don't mean to do that. And I'm Seth."

"Seth." She smiled and crossed her legs.

Seth cleared his throat. "Claire...ma'am, I'm sorry to have to tell you that your grandfather has passed away." He stared at her, waiting for her reaction, hand creeping toward his breast pocket where she suspected he had a white handkerchief at the ready.

He thought she didn't know. No wonder he was so somber. "Yes," she said, subdued. "I know."

In an instant, his sympathetic expression vanished and his head reared back like an angry stallion's. "You *know*?"

Claire nodded.

Seth straightened, both hands on his knees, anger evident. "And you couldn't be bothered to come to the funeral? At least you could've responded to the letters the lawyers sent you." He shook his head. "That's cold, ma'am, really cold."

Stung, Claire defended herself. "For your information, I received the letters less than an hour ago!"

"They were overnighted last week!"

"I hadn't made it to my post office box. Anyway, couldn't somebody have been bothered to pick up a telephone and call me?" She deliberately echoed his word choice.

"We tried. You aren't listed."

"True," Claire shot back. "But Beau had my number." He'd never used it. Claire had always been the one to call him, and she hadn't done that too often.

"No one could find it."

"Then why didn't you call me here at the shop?" Claire was on the offensive, now. How dare this stranger chastise her? "You obviously knew where I worked."

"We didn't until after the funeral." The hard set of his mouth relaxed somewhat. "Truth to tell, I was mad and wanted to fly here and see for myself the kind of granddaughter who'd shun her kin."

"Shun my kin?" One minute he sounded like a sophisticate and the next he was a good ol' country boy. Either way, he had no business judging her. "You flew here just because you thought I'd ignored my grandfather?"

"I call 'em like I see 'em."

Claire narrowed her eyes. "Look, I had to sign for those letters. If you'd checked with your lawyers, they'd have told you they hadn't received the delivery confirmation yet." She guessed that he hadn't asked about the confirmation before he'd come flying to New York in outrage. Seth Montgomery was obviously an impatient man.

But not a closed-minded one. "You've got me there." He twirled his hat between his hands.

And as long as he was finally on the defensive, Claire wanted to press her advantage. "Flying on a moment's notice is expensive. I'm sure you just discovered that, right?"

This time when he raised the corner of his mouth, Claire knew it was a smile. For such a tiny movement, it entirely changed his expression. Creases along the sides of his mouth deepened, and his eyes warmed, prompting a warming trend in Claire, as well.

She decided that she'd have to rethink her bias against cowboy types. "You shouldn't be so quick to condemn people. The only way I could have afforded to come to the funeral is because I've got money I've been saving for something else. Other people might not."

"You're right," he capitulated easily. "I owe you an apology. And also my condolences."

Claire nodded regally, a little surprised that he was apparently over his anger so quickly. It was almost as if he wanted to get on her good side, but she couldn't fathom why.

"Sorry you wasted a trip to New York," she said, when she became uncomfortable under his steady gaze.

"It wasn't a waste. I wanted to meet you anyway."

"Why on earth would you want to meet me?" Claire was too astonished to be coy.

"Well, under the circumstances and all." He smiled. "Beau talked about you some."

"He *did*?" Now she really felt guilty. She should have written more. Called more.

"You sound surprised."

"I am," Claire admitted. "We weren't particularly close, not like some families. I'd only met him once before the time I came to stay with him that summer my parents were divorced. Beau and I kept in touch—which is more than I can say for my father. I never saw him again."

Seth shifted on the chair. "I understand Beau's son is deceased."

"Yes." And that was all Claire planned to say about her father. "And I missed his funeral, too."

She gazed steadily at Seth, challenging him to comment on her lack of feeling.

He stared at her, one eye slightly narrowed. "You should check your mail more often."

There hadn't been mail that time. She'd been away at school, and her mother simply hadn't informed her until later. "I've been working night and day on a project. I finished it this morning and checked my mail for the first time in a week. I'm sorry I missed the funeral. Truly. Are you satisfied now?"

Seth stared at his hat. "We can't change what's in the past. Time to move on." He met her eyes again. "Can you be ready to fly to Texas tomorrow morning, or should I make reservations for later?"

"What?"

"If you can be ready to leave tomorrow, I'll fly back with you," he offered. "Three days are my limit for being away from my ranch. Otherwise, you'll have to come on your own, and I'll send a car to take you to Bellingham from the airport."

"But..." He probably thought she'd want to see her relatives or something. The poor man must be really shocked by the unfeeling Bellingham clan. "Since I've missed the funeral, why should I go to

Texas? If I've got relatives there, it's a little late to make their acquaintance now."

Seth started to say something, but Claire cut him off. "Look, Beau and my father quarreled when he left the ranch. For years, I didn't even know I *had* a grandfather. And it's only through him that I know I've got cousins, but I've never seen them and they certainly haven't made any effort to contact me."

"They will be," Seth muttered under his breath.

Claire touched his arm. "You must have been a good friend to my grandfather and you'll think I'm awful, but it won't make any difference to him now if I fly to Texas, and it *will* make a huge difference in my financial situation." Claire's voice broke. She felt horrible and guilty and she wished she could just whip out a charge card and fly to Texas on a moment's notice with this compelling rancher. But she'd gone without in order to save enough to finance her study in Paris, and blowing all her savings on a trip to the ranch just to keep up appearances was asking too much of her.

Her throat tightened, and she was afraid she was going to cry. She didn't want to cry now. She wanted to wait until tonight when she could say goodbye to Beau in her own way—by rereading his letters alone in her bedroom.

She swallowed and blinked.

Into her field of vision, a large white square appeared. At the same time, she felt Seth's callused hand grip her shoulder.

"Thanks," she managed and took the handkerchief, though she was determined not to ruin it with her makeup.

He sighed and stood. "I'd hoped to be able to bring you back with me. It would sure make things easier—and quicker. And whenever you're dealing with lawyers, quicker is less expensive."

"Yeah." Claire stood, too, and she still had to look a long way up at him. She returned his handkerchief, pleased that she hadn't needed it.

They walked toward the door in silence. Once there, Seth withdrew a gold card case from his pocket, extracted a business card and handed it to her. "As soon as you feel up to the trip, give me a call and I'll send a car to the airport in Austin for you. And if you could possibly make it by the end of the week, I'd appreciate it." He nodded and put on his hat. "Things are pretty much at a standstill until you get there."

"But why?"

Seth looked at her, his brows drawn together. "Well, because of the ranch situation."

"What about it? I've never had anything to do with the ranch."

He stared at her. "Didn't Beau..." Seth exhaled slowly, his eyes closed.

Claire had a feeling that if she hadn't been standing there, Seth would have been swearing.

He opened his eyes. "Claire, with Beau's passing, you're the new owner of Bellingham Ranch."

CHAPTER TWO

CLAIRE hadn't believed him. But why would he lie?

Still, she'd called the law firm, and they'd told her enough to convince her that whether or not she inherited all or part of Bellingham Ranch, there was sufficient unfinished business to warrant a trip to Texas.

Which was why she now found herself being driven by Seth down a two-lane blacktop in the middle of the Texas Hill country.

It was the tail end of the wildflower season. A threadbare blanket of bluebonnets and Indian paintbrush stretched over the fields and the sides of the road.

Other than the flowers, the countryside was much the same as she remembered from that dreadful summer fifteen years ago. Gentle hills and scrubby bushes, creamy rocks and compact live oaks. Every so often, an ornate iron arch over a dirt road off the main highway marked the entrance to another of the small ranches so prevalent in this area. A mailbox always grew beside the gate, and an unprepossessing ranch house generally sat under the only clump of trees for miles around.

Though it was only April, it was fiercely hot. Claire wore a black suit with suede over-the-knee boots. She'd agonized about the proper dress for this trip. Appearances were obviously of the utmost importance to Seth and the others, whoever they were.

Already in disgrace because she'd missed her grandfather's funeral, Claire decided wearing black would show the proper respect, thereby soothing any ruffled feathers. On the other hand, she didn't want people to accuse her of appearing phony with a theatrical show of mourning.

Besides, black made her look thin. She wore lots of black. Thus, she decided on the fashionable boots to give her outfit a certain élan. Fashionable respect, as it were.

And now her fashionable feet were sweltering. The air-conditioning in the Jeep Cherokee hummed but was no match for sun streaming through windows onto black wool. Claire leaned against the door to catch the flow of air from the vent.

"You cool enough?" Seth asked, breaking miles of silence.

"I'm fine," she lied.

Seth's suit jacket was spread over the backseat, along with his hat. His white shirt was Western cut, and instead of a tie, he wore a string bolo with a silver clip. And Wrangler jeans. He looked entirely at ease. Entirely in his element.

Claire felt entirely too New Yorkish, an appearance she'd always strived for but never felt she quite succeeded in attaining.

As a child, she'd lived in a lot of places, but most of them were in the North and Northeast. She was used to men in suits and regular ties, and seasons in their proper place. Eighty-eight degrees in April, indeed.

She slid a sideways look at Seth and wondered what he thought of her. Probably that she was an unfeeling money grubber, which she wasn't. Or an undeserving city slicker, which she was.

Honestly, though, Claire didn't want her grandfather's ranch. She wanted to continue her life in New York City, or, if she won her scholarship, in Paris. She wanted to be a fashion designer, and it had been slow going so far.

Closing her eyes, she rested her head against the car window. This trip to Texas, in spite of the sad circumstances, would be a welcome break between the pressure of assembling her contest entry and gearing up for the holiday season. Audrey had a stable of regular clients who wanted something unique for the holidays and were willing to pay for it. Claire always garnered several commissions for holiday outfits, which added to her Paris fund.

Unfortunately, to pay for this trip, she'd subtracted from her Paris fund. She'd have to work harder than ever this year, she thought with a sigh.

"You can use my jacket as a pillow, if you like." Seth's voice jerked her away from her thoughts.

Claire opened her eyes and turned in her seat so she could face him. "Why is it that travel is so exhausting? All we do is sit."

Seth chuckled. He had a nice laugh. In fact, Claire thought with an appraising look, he had a nice face. And shoulders and torso. In fact, cowboy types were beginning to appeal to her. It must be the Texas heat.

She unbuttoned the two lower buttons of her long skirt, hoping to catch some cooler air.

Seth reached in front of her and kicked the air-conditioning up a notch.

"Thanks," Claire said, abandoning her pretense of comfort.

"You should have said something."

"I didn't want to be a bother—any more than I've already been," she added.

"You haven't been a bother." Seth's tone indicated that he'd expected her to be. He glanced toward her. "And I appreciate you coming here to put things right."

Just before he turned his attention back to the road, she caught him glancing at the undone buttons at the hem of her slim skirt.

Claire crossed her legs, feeling immeasurably more cheerful. The third button pulled a bit, so she slipped it out of the buttonhole. Two inches of skin gleamed whitely above her boots. *Like that's really going to drive him wild, Claire.* He probably wouldn't even notice. "At the risk of sounding childish, when will we get there?"

"In about thirty or forty more minutes," Seth answered.

Claire looked out at the passing land. Clumps of cattle huddled under the few trees, and rows of green striped the fields. "I don't recognize any of this."

"When were you last here?"

Claire thought back. "I was thirteen, so it's been fifteen years." If he bothered to do the math, he'd know how old she was. He was older, or seemed older. She wondered just how much, but couldn't figure out a clever way to ask without being obvious.

"Nothing much has changed in these parts, though Bellingham might look a bit different."

"How so?"

Seth lifted a shoulder. "Beau reduced his herd after the drought. Most of us did."

Claire searched her memory for anything about a drought. All she could remember from her grandfather's twice-yearly letters was a comment or two about a "hard year." It seemed like all the years were "hard years," including her own. "I never was around the cows much that summer," she said. "I . . . they were so big, and I'm not much of an animal lover."

Was it her imagination, or did Seth wince? She led the subject away from Bellingham Ranch. "Have you always lived on your ranch?"

"Except when I was away at school, yes." He shifted in his seat, as if settling in. "My great-grandfather settled the place. My grandparents lived on the ranch and then my father. He's gone now, but my mother still lives there and works as hard as ever."

Seth was stating facts, not complaining, Claire surmised. He may have been born into ranching, but he was obviously his own man. The question was, was he also somebody else's man?

Claire tilted her head until she could see his hands on the steering wheel. He wore no wedding ring, or any other ring, but there was no law that forced a married man to wear a wedding ring.

There should be, though.

"Tell me about your ranch—how far is it from Bellingham?"

"We're neighbors to the southeast."

"Close neighbors?"

He smiled. "As close as close gets out here."

That sounded promising. If his place bordered Bellingham, then he'd be a logical buyer for her grandfather's ranch. She eyed Seth speculatively. Maybe that's why he flew to New York to fetch her—he wanted to beat the competition.

Claire didn't mind. She was probably the most motivated seller this part of Texas had ever seen. If Seth wanted to buy, more power to him. All she wanted to do was go back to New York.

"So, do you have a big place?" That could stand to get bigger?

"I've got a fairly nice spread. The Montgomery Rose is about twice the size of Bellingham, but Bellingham has got some prime growing land."

Aha. Quality over quantity. Small, but fertile. She'd have to remember to tell the real estate agent that. But if Seth was interested in buying, maybe she wouldn't even have to put the place on the market.

A ringing telephone interrupted her thoughts. "Could you get my phone out of my jacket pocket?" Seth asked.

Claire stared at him. "You've got a cellular phone?"

It rang again, making her question sound stupid.

"Of course. They're handy little things. Don't you have one?"

"No." She couldn't afford one.

Claire twisted around until she could reach his jacket. The lapel opened, revealing the label of a contemporary men's designer. Perhaps the jacket wasn't from this season, but quality was quality. As Claire handed Seth his telephone, she reflected that perhaps Texas wasn't quite the unsophisticated frontier she'd remembered it as.

Lost in her thoughts, she paid no attention to Seth's conversation and was caught unaware when he spoke to her.

"Claire, is that okay with you?"

"What?"

"The legal team can meet with you about four-thirty today, if you're up to it. They offered to drive out."

"Of course they did, they're being paid by the hour, aren't they?" Good grief, if that's the way the ranchers were doing business out here, she was surprised her grandfather had any kind of estate left.

Seth raised an eyebrow, and Claire belatedly understood that her remarks must have been overheard. Embarrassed, she signaled her agreement to the meeting.

"Four-thirty is fine, Aaron." Seth flipped his phone closed and set it on the console between them.

Claire took one look at his forbidding expression and inwardly sighed. The lawyers were probably personal friends of his. Well, didn't she remember a conversation when he'd said quicker was cheaper and used it as the reason she had to come to Texas?

She started to remind him, then changed her mind and offered an apology. "Sorry if I offended you. I guess I've overheard too many conversations about billable hours while I've stood in line at the deli. This group of lawyers always ate there. They'd mention a case and then laugh about writing the whole time off to some poor client."

"I think you'll find Alexander and Hawthorne is a reputable firm," Seth commented in his deep voice.

Claire felt put in her place.

"We need to swing by my place for some papers. Do you mind?"

"No." In fact, Claire wanted to see the Montgomery Rose.

Seth slowed the Jeep, pulled to the side and then U-turned. "The road is a couple of miles back."

Everything was measured in miles out here. Claire was used to city blocks.

A discreet wooden sign announced the direction of the Montgomery Rose. Seth turned onto the road, and Claire began looking for the ranch house. All around she saw fields and nothing else. They drove for what seemed miles and miles until the fencing changed from barbed wire to white wood, and a huge open gate appeared with Montgomery Rose arched over the drive.

Still no ranch house that Claire could see.

And then they drove over a slight hill and there it was.

She gasped. A cluster of pristine buildings sat among enormous shade trees. "*That's* your ranch?"

"We've been driving on the Montgomery Rose for a spell, yes," Seth confirmed, pride in his voice.

From what she remembered of Bellingham, Seth's ranch was considerably larger.

"Is that the ranch house?" Claire pointed to a sprawling one-story Spanish-style house next to a duck pond.

"Yes. I'd stop and introduce you to my mother, but I'm not sure she's there and I'm not sure we've got time," he apologized. "I just need to run into the office."

Since he drove right by the house, Claire surmised that the ranch offices were located in one of the separate buildings.

Seth headed for a smaller, tan barracks-style building that boasted its own asphalt parking lot. True, it was a small lot, but the fact that there was one at all spoke volumes.

"Be right back," he said, parking the Cherokee. "You can wait here, or come inside to stretch your legs."

She was curious to see the inside of a ranch office. Her grandfather just had a desk in his bedroom. "I'll come inside."

A smiling, middle-aged woman looked up from her computer as they entered. "Seth, you're back!" She whirled around and grabbed a stack of pink messages slips.

"Technically, I'm not back yet, Viv. Pretend you haven't seen me." He held up his hands to shield his face and, accompanied by her laughter, hurried past her. "This is Claire Bellingham," he called just before disappearing into his office.

"Hello," Viv greeted Claire, her voice turning serious. "I was sorry to hear about your grandfather."

"Thank you." Feeling awkward, Claire gave her a solemn nod and followed Seth into his office.

Although Claire had never been in a ranch office, it looked just the way she might imagine a rancher's office to look. Dark paneling, hefty wooden furniture, chocolate leather chairs and walls covered with plaques.

While Seth pulled open a file cabinet, Claire read the plaques. Most were acknowledging Montgomery Rose's contributions to local 4-H clubs and the scholarships offered by the Houston Livestock Show and Rodeo. Some of the plaques were older than she was. "You're quite the philanthropist."

He shrugged and pulled out a file folder. "I try to do my part."

"Looks like it's been a big part." She gestured to the wall.

An unconscious pride settled over his features as he gazed at the plaques. "My grandfather started the tradition and my dad and I kept it up. It's part of being a Montgomery."

Claire, who had never lived in one place for very long, couldn't imagine what it must be like to have roots as deep as Seth's, or such a sense of family. To her, Bellingham was just a name.

She would have liked to linger in his office, but Seth appeared at her side. "Ready to go?"

Outside, Claire looked around before getting into the Jeep. "You've got a significant operation here."

He grinned. "It's home."

Right. Seth just wasn't a humble cowboy. He was, in effect, the CEO of a corporation.

"I guess I didn't realize ranching was such a modern business," Claire said as they pulled away from the office.

"It has to be. Now my father recognized that, but a lot of the folks around here are doing things the way they've always done."

And weren't succeeding, Claire guessed.

Within thirty minutes, they arrived at Bellingham. Having just come from Seth's ranch, Claire couldn't help contrasting the two.

As with most of the small ranches in the area, Bellingham boasted an iron arch over the roadway. On either side of the word Bellingham was the outline of a bell, which Claire remembered was the brand on the cattle. But that was about the only thing Bellingham had in common with the Montgomery Rose.

There weren't any cattle in the fields next to the highway. Claire supposed they were grazing in a distant pasture or that someone else was taking care of them.

Her grandfather had just added onto the barn, Claire saw. Lumber was still stacked next to it, and the new part hadn't even been painted yet.

As Seth drove up the roadway, paved now, but dirt when Claire had visited, she stared at the single-story stone ranch house. And for the first time understood what had compelled her father to leave his family home—the isolation.

She'd forgotten how insular ranch life could be. This was no Montgomery Rose, with multiple buildings and lots of people. Other than seasonal ranch personnel and family, there was no one to talk to and nothing but chores to do. The nearest neighbor wasn't even in sight. Toward the end of the summer, Claire had welcomed trips into Royerville, the nearest town, even though they generally meant trips to the doctor and allergy shots.

Claire was a people person. Maybe her father had been, too. For the first time, Claire thought she understood a little about her father—this part, anyway. But understanding was a long way from forgiving, and Claire didn't feel like forgiving the man who divorced not only his wife, but his daughter, as well.

Seth parked next to a couple of pickup trucks in the circular drive in front of the ranch house. "That'll be Pete Stevens and Luke Chance."

"The lawyers?"

"Nope," Seth said and opened the car door. "Two of the other ranchers in the partnership."

Weren't they going to give her any time to collect herself? These Texas ranchers were an impatient lot.

After all, this was Bellingham. Presumably she would be considered the hostess, and she had no idea of the state of the house or the kitchen.

Boots crunching, Seth walked around to her side and opened the door.

Swinging her legs out of the car onto the white crushed gravel drive, Claire sighed as dust instantly powdered her black suede boots. Great.

She didn't have time to dwell on her less than elegant appearance because the front door opened and two men hailed Seth.

"Hey, Seth! Did you corral that filly?"

"Got her right here." He slapped the side of the car and grinned.

Claire stayed put. "I am not a horse." No one heard her.

"Hey, no foolin'?" The older rancher, a grizzled cowboy type, turned to the younger man, one who could hold his own with Seth in the tough-hombre category. "Luke, you owe me a steak dinner!"

"I'll admit I'm surprised, Seth." Luke shook his head. "New Yorkers can be mighty stubborn."

"I'd guess you'd know, since you married one," Seth retorted.

The older man continued to cackle. "He said he was going to do it, and by gum, he did it!"

"I am not a horse," Claire repeated, grasping that there must have been some sort of bet about whether Seth could coax her to Texas. "And I do not wish to be referred to as one."

Seth finally noticed that she wasn't getting out of the car. "Did you say something?" He ducked until he could see into the car.

"I *said* that I'm not a horse!"

Seth blinked. The afternoon sun shone in his face, and his eyelashes cast shadows on his cheeks. "Ma'am—Claire, no one has called you a horse."

"*He*—" she pointed "—said filly."

"Well, yes, ma'am, I suppose he did, but he didn't mean to be disrespectful."

Privately, Claire thought that was exactly what the old rancher had meant, but she had made her point, and it wasn't necessary to grind it into the dust. Accepting the hand Seth offered, she exited the car as gracefully as she could. Unfortunately, her boot heels sank into the gravel, doing heaven knew what damage to the suede.

Her skirt, in spite of the three undone buttons, was too narrow to allow a wide stride. Wobbling her way across the drive under the scrutiny of three men, Claire wondered why her grandfather had paved the road, but not the drive.

Three steps led to the porch. As Seth bounded up, they squeaked and sagged.

Claire stopped. A quick glance around revealed that the wooden trim and porch were badly in need of paint. Cracks appeared in the stone mortar, and a trellis next to the porch was weathered nearly gray. Just enough white paint remained on the protected side next to the house to tell her that the whole thing should be white.

Apparently her grandfather's ranch house was a real fixer-upper. He should have been repairing it instead of adding to the barn. Well, if Seth wanted the place, it would be for the land and not the ranch house.

Seth pulled open the screen door with a screech that made the fillings in her molars vibrate. Still, Claire felt encouraged as she preceded the men into the house. Maybe if Seth didn't want the ranch, one of the others would.

The spring in the door snapped it closed, and Claire was transported back in time fifteen years.

The same furniture was in exactly the same arrangement. The same ugly olive green, tan and yellow canvas leaf print covered two chairs, a sofa and the window curtains. Too bad the stuff had apparently worn like iron.

The area rug hadn't, though, Claire noticed as she walked forward to drop her purse onto the couch. It was worn and sun-faded along the edge next to the window, and chunks of fringe had been gnawed away. "Blackie," she whispered as she toed a bare spot.

"You remember that old dog?" asked the older man.

Claire had momentarily forgotten the men, who'd stood behind her in silence. "Yes, he was alive when I was here."

She smiled at them, waiting to be introduced.

Seth smoothly picked up his cue. Indicating the older man, he said, "Claire, this is Pete Stevens."

Pete nodded. "Ma'am."

"And Luke Chance."

Another nod and another ma'am.

"Please call me Claire," she said, conscious that Seth was still struggling to do so.

"I'm very sorry about your grandfather," Luke said. "Beau was a fine man."

"One of the best," added Pete.

Claire murmured, wishing she didn't feel so awkward, wishing she felt entitled to all these expressions of sympathy. She wondered if Seth had told them why she missed the funeral.

She met his eyes and he smiled gently. "I'll bring in your luggage."

"Need some help?" Luke offered.

Seth shook his head, and a look passed among the three of them.

What was that all about? Claire wondered. She'd brought one suitcase, for heaven's sake! No man could complain about that.

"I'd offer you something to drink," she said to the two men as the screen slapped shut behind Seth, "but I don't know what there is to offer."

"Root beer," the men chorused.

"Your granddaddy was mighty fond of root beer," Pete reminisced.

Root beer. She hadn't drunk root beer since that summer.

"Root beer it is, then." Claire remembered the way to the huge kitchen. During her sojourn at the ranch, one of her responsibilities had been to help Mrs. Deeves, the cook, with the kitchen chores.

The kitchen had a long table where workers ate meals and where she could see Pete and Luke had been sitting. Claire poured a round of root beers as Seth returned, followed by two more men.

They, too, wore jeans, shirts and boots and had telltale indentations in their hair left by cowboy hats.

How many ranchers were in the partnership, anyway? Claire wondered.

But Seth introduced these men as the lawyers. "I put your bag in the back bedroom," he told her in an undertone.

"Good. I want my notebook out of it."

After offering root beer to the lawyers, Claire excused herself and headed down the hall.

The ranch house had three bedrooms and two bathrooms. Claire automatically turned into the room where she'd stayed before. Seth had put her suitcase on the bed. Smiling, Claire wondered if he'd guessed this was the room she'd used or if it was a coincidence.

She flipped open the latches on her suitcase, then withdrew the notebook and her cosmetic case. With all the males in the kitchen, Claire felt a need to refresh her makeup.

She carried her bag to the vanity and stopped. There, in a silver frame, was a picture of her thirteen-year-old self on a horse.

Her grandfather had kept a picture of her on display? Touched, Claire picked it up. In the picture, she was smiling—it had been early in the summer, before her allergies had made her so miserable.

Well, she was prepared this trip. Her purse was packed with medicines to battle the pollen and animals, not that she planned a long stay.

She replaced the picture on the crocheted doily covering the vanity top, then ran a comb through her short bob, reapplied red lipstick and decided she was ready to do business.

She picked up her notebook and walked out of the room, then halted and slowly reversed her steps, hesitating on the threshold of her grandfather's room.

How perceptive of Seth not to have carried her suitcase in here. Her grandfather might be gone, but this was still his room.

The bed was neatly made, but an open book and a glass sat on the nightstand. His watch, a pocketknife and change from his pocket were scattered on top of the dresser.

And her high school graduation picture sat in an oval frame. It wasn't alone—two other of the formal graduation portraits were next to it. Curious, Claire walked over to study them. A boy and a girl. They must be her cousins, though she'd never met them.

But now was not the time to dwell on it. There would be plenty of time later. Abruptly, she wheeled around and walked to the kitchen. The ranchers were waiting on her. Lawyers were present. Time was money.

Plastering a confident smile onto her face, she took a place at the head of the table. She would have preferred to sit elsewhere, but the men were lined up on either side, brown root beer bottles standing at attention.

Seth was on her right. "The other two partners weren't able to get away," he said, "so we can start any time you're ready."

"I'm ready," Claire said, and opened her notebook.

But she quickly learned that she wasn't ready. Certainly not to hear that her grandfather had, indeed, left everything to her. She couldn't believe it.

"I just don't understand," she said when one of the lawyers had finished reading the pertinent parts of the will. "What about my cousins or any other relatives?"

The ranchers all looked at each other and then at the table. All, that is, except Seth. He glanced at Claire and then nodded to the lawyers.

"Will you quit doing that?" Claire burst out. "There is obviously something I don't know—starting with the fact that this is all a complete surprise to me. Beau never said a word. Never. And somehow, you're all involved or you wouldn't be here. Just tell me and let me deal with it."

Following her outburst, there was a lot of throat clearing and paper shuffling, which irritated her even more. She threw her pen down and crossed her arms. "Talk, somebody."

"Miss Bellingham," began one of the lawyers.

Claire didn't ask him to use her first name.

Seth broke in. "Your cousins opposed the ostrich venture. They thought Beau was too old to be investing in a new business. He disagreed. So they went to court to have Beau declared incompetent."

Everyone looked at her. "I had no idea." About that or anything else. It was painfully obvious. They must wonder what on earth Beau had been thinking. Claire certainly was.

"They were unsuccessful," said the older of the lawyers with a dry smile. "However, we suggested Beau make provisions for the ranch in the event of his untimely demise, which has unfortunately come to pass."

"He never said a word about leaving me the ranch," Claire reiterated.

"I doubt Beau thought it would come to this," Seth replied.

"Well, I might as well tell you that I have no intention of taking up ranching. I'm a designer. I live in New York. I'm planning to study in Paris. So, the ranch is for sale. Seth, or any of you who wants to make an offer..." Claire shrugged and gestured toward the lawyers. "Will you handle the paperwork for me?"

There was silence. And another round of everybody meeting everybody's eyes but Claire's. What now?

Seth nodded toward the legal team. "Go on, Aaron, tell her the rest."

The older lawyer, Aaron, shifted papers. "Miss Bellingham, there is a condition to your inheritance. It was Beau's wish to support the ostrich partnership."

"I have no problem with that." Unless it involved her personal funds, but she'd set them straight about *that* real fast.

"Therefore," he continued, ignoring her, "you will inherit the ranch after you have lived on it for a period of not less than one year."

CHAPTER THREE

"YOU'RE telling me that I have to live here for a year to inherit this place?"

"That is the condition as set forth in the will," Aaron intoned.

"There must be some mistake," Claire stated flatly. "I have a job and a life in New York. Beau knew that." She looked around the room and saw that everyone was staring at Seth. "Did *you* have something to do with this?" she asked him.

Seth shifted forward, both hands wrapped around the root beer bottle. He stared at it, tracing the condensation with his thumb. "Since I'm head of this venture, Beau did discuss with me who would look out for his interests if he couldn't." Seth gazed at her, his lips curved in a humorless smile. "It came down to you or the Bellingham branch who thought he was nuts. He chose you."

"Well, how does he know *I* don't think he's nuts? Frankly, picking a New York fashion designer who's allergic to Texas to run his ranch strikes me as a questionable business decision."

"That was my idea," Seth stated calmly.

"Then *you're* nuts!"

Seth's jaw was set, and he glanced a challenge around the table. No one dared say anything, though everyone immediately took a swallow of root beer.

Claire didn't have any root beer. She wished she did. It was obvious that the lawyers and ranchers sitting at this table regarded Seth as their leader. They'd deferred to him ever since Claire had arrived. And now she'd insulted him.

These men weren't like the men she was used to in New York. The veneer of civilization was thinner in Texas. These men dealt with life on a more elemental level than she was used to. Rather than fight with words, they'd fight with action.

Even so, it behooved her not to underestimate any of them. The lawyers, for instance. They might dress country and they might talk country, but Claire recognized a manicure when she saw one.

The atmosphere of the ranch house kitchen had changed. Though the men would take their cue from Seth, Claire could feel waves of disapproval emanating from them.

She turned to find him regarding her impassively. "You don't actually expect me to live here, do you?"

She'd addressed Seth, but Aaron answered. "If you want to inherit the ranch—"

Seth lifted his hand, and the lawyer ceased talking immediately.

Claire took note. Seth was definitely considered to be in charge around here. But she wasn't from around here, was she?

"Unfortunately, your grandfather picked a mighty inconvenient time to die," he said.

"How inconsiderate of him," Claire snapped, appalled. Her grandfather had died, and these men were upset about being inconvenienced!

Seth ignored her. "We need the resources of Bellingham to meet the commitments the partnership has made. Beau's purpose in leaving you the ranch was to see that plans continue with a minimum of disruption.''

''I understand,'' Claire said, speaking calmly and deliberately, ''but I also have plans that I want to continue with a minimum of disruption. Therefore, why don't I just sell the ranch to you. Any of you.'' She included the room at large. ''I guarantee it'll be the bargain of the century.''

''Miss Bellingham.'' Aaron whispered to the lawyer next to him and waited as the man withdrew papers from a file. ''What you must understand is that you cannot dispose of the ranch, nor take possession of it, until the terms of the inheritance have been fulfilled.''

''You mean I can't sell the ranch?''

''Not at this time,'' the lawyer said, shaking his head as he leafed through the papers. ''Not until you've lived here for at least one year.''

Unbelievable. This was like some archaic provision of the Middle Ages. ''Beau should have said something to me.''

But he hadn't. If he had, she'd have told him she didn't want the ranch. *Didn't want the ranch*. Maybe that was a way out.

''Isn't there a letter for her or something?'' Seth asked Aaron.

''Not to my knowledge.''

Taking a deep breath, Seth turned to her. ''Claire,'' he began.

But Claire had thought of something. ''If I can't sell the ranch, then I'll give it away.''

She smiled as she watched the expressions on the faces of the men. Priceless. Clearly, she'd caught them off-guard. It was a lovely, satisfying feeling.

But it didn't last.

"Miss Bellingham." Sighing, Aaron again shook his head, a patronizing tone in his voice. "You can't give it away. You can't dispose of the property until you've—"

"Lived on the ranch for a year. Yes, so you've said." Claire tapped her pen on her notebook. She hadn't written anything yet. "What happens if I *don't* live here... fulfill the terms of the inheritance, as I believe you refer to the situation?"

Oh, that possibility bothered them. Pete began muttering to himself. Luke and Seth stared at each other, and the lawyers shuffled papers. These men should never play poker. Or perhaps they should. With her.

"Well? My cousins get the ranch and cause all sorts of trouble, right?"

"No." Aaron held out his hand and received another set of papers. "The entire ranch will go to Texas A&M University. But according to Texas law, you have nine months in which to decline the inheritance."

"I do?" No one had mentioned that. She raised an eyebrow in Seth's direction.

Mouth set, he stood abruptly, scraping the chair across the tile. "I want to talk with Claire in private." He held out his hand, which Claire automatically grasped, realizing that protesting would be counter-productive—and probably ignored.

He nodded to the room. "The rest of y'all make yourselves at home."

Claire stood and found herself maneuvered out of the kitchen, through the front room and onto the porch before she quite realized what was happening.

On their way out, Seth plucked a hat from among several on the hat tree to the left of the front door.

"Is this where you put the pressure on?" Claire asked as the screen door slammed shut.

"Yes," he responded bluntly and shoved his hands into the back pockets of his jeans.

A late-afternoon breeze puffed through the leaves of a big old live oak in the front yard. Silence reigned. "Where are the animals?" she asked. She hadn't heard a moo or a whinny or a cluck since she'd arrived.

"The cattle are mostly gone. Beau just has a few head left. I'm boarding the horses at my place. Pete's wife is feeding your chickens."

Her chickens. Claire shuddered. This life was not for her, and she had to make Seth understand. "Seth, I don't want the ranch. I never expected to inherit it, so it's no loss to me. And I certainly don't want to live here. Look at me." She gestured to herself, at the sleek black wool suit and the suede boots, dusty but unmistakably expensive. "I'm not a ranch person. I have a job, one that I love, and I want to get back to it. There's nothing you can offer me here."

"I don't know about that." Walking to the edge of the porch, Seth gazed out across the fallow fields. "What is it you want?"

"To go back to New York."

"No." He turned and leaned against the railing. "I mean, what do you *want*. Out of life. Money?"

"Doesn't everybody?"

He shrugged. "Say you had money... what would you do with it?"

"Go to Paris," she said at once. "To study. To learn." She joined him at the railing, grabbing it with both hands and leaning back. "To live. To absorb.

To create.'' Just the thought of Paris made her beam. ''I've been working toward that goal ever since I got out of school. And Beau knew it.''

''So why haven't you gone?'' Seth asked. ''That's an awful long time to be wanting something so bad.''

''Money, of course.''

Seth nodded, as if something had become clear to him. ''Claire, did you ever think that leaving you the ranch might be Beau's way of helping you get to Paris?''

''By tying me here?''

''Well, that's on account of the ostriches.''

''You know,'' Claire said, pointedly looking around, ''I don't see any ostriches.''

''C'mon. Let me show you what we've got planned.'' He started down the steps, apparently unconcerned about their stability, and waited impatiently at the bottom.

As Claire gingerly descended, Seth took off across the gravel, footfalls crunching.

Wincing for her boots, Claire tromped after him. With each step, gravel bit into the two-inch heels, no doubt gouging the suede. *If he thinks he's getting any points after ruining an expensive pair of boots . . .*

Seth noticed that she wasn't keeping up and slowed his loping stride. He glanced back at the precise moment Claire's ankle wobbled and she stumbled. He was at her side in a flash.

''Grab on,'' he said, offering his arm.

''Gladly.'' Claire clutched it, feeling rock-solid muscles she knew he hadn't acquired in any expensive health club.

She was impressed, though why, she didn't know. The man worked outside, he *should* have muscles. She worked inside, therefore she did *not* have muscles. And never the twain should meet. She'd do well to remember that and not get any foolish ideas about dallying with Texas cowboys.

The Texas cowboy was speaking. "You might remember this as the horse barn." They'd stopped in front of the largest building other than the ranch house.

"I remember." Claire's nose twitched, but she'd been taking her allergy medicine. What a test it was about to get.

"Beau added on to it for the ostrich hatchery. The incubators will be in the old part and the hatchery will be in the add-on."

Claire pointed to the piles of lumber. "Doesn't look as though he finished."

"Not quite. He was going to build a couple of small sheds for the chicks, but that wasn't critical—" he glanced at her "— then."

"And now I suppose it is?"

Seth nodded as they reached the barn. Claire dropped her hand as he pulled open the creaking double door.

Boy, this place brought back memories. Claire had been determined to care for the horse Beau had let her ride for the summer, but personality wise, she and the horse weren't a good match. Claire didn't know how to ride, and the horse wasn't inclined toward patience. Even worse was the currying, when Claire's inexperience with the combs and brushes pulled the horse's hair.

But as Seth flipped on the lights, Claire saw the barn was empty. Only a faint musty odor lingered, telling her that horses hadn't lived here in awhile. "I guess things were worse than I thought," she murmured into the silence.

"Yes and no," Seth replied, kicking debris out of her path. "It's hard for midsize ranchers to make a living these days, especially after the drought and the cold we had during the winter. The price of winter feed skyrocketed. And we've had a real wet spring, which always causes problems."

"But there's nothing here." She turned to him. "Why do I need to stay? There aren't any animals, no crops . . . I don't get it."

"The group of us, including your grandfather, got hit hard. Frankly, I don't see that the situation for independent ranches is going to improve. The big spreads are run by corporations, and we can't compete." Seth warmed to the topic, and his deep voice took on the practiced oratory of a tent preacher. "People in these parts are losing ranches that have been in their families for generations. If we're going to keep our ranches, we've got to change the way we do business."

Claire expected him to smack his fist into his palm. He didn't. "You sound like you're giving a speech."

Seth gave her a wry smile. "Actually, I have."

"That one?"

"Yeah." he grinned. "It worked before, and I thought, why waste good material?"

Claire chuckled and brushed at a piece of hay clinging to her skirt. "So you convinced everybody to invest in ostriches."

"They didn't take much convincing when I showed them the projected profit. Come on back here."

Following Seth to the new section of the barn, Claire passed through dust-laden sunbeams that shone through the slats in the side of the barn. She sneezed, probably due more to the power of suggestion than because she really needed to.

It was hot and stuffy in the barn, but Seth's white shirt was as crisp as when they left New York this morning.

How did he do that? Claire fanned her face and sighed. She wore wool, silk and suede. Natural materials had never felt so unnatural.

"We've converted the back part of the barn to hold the incubators, and this new part will have the hatchers." Seth indicated places where stalls had once been.

She followed him into the room, which had tables, a complicated-looking boxy piece of machinery, heat lamps and a sink. "It looks like a nursery."

"That's exactly what it is," he said. "Because Beau was getting on in years and wasn't interested in working cattle anymore, we were going to bring eggs here and he'd take care of them and the young chicks."

"And that's what you want me to do? Baby-sit a bunch of eggs?"

"No."

"Sounds like it to me."

With an exasperated scowl, Seth grabbed two large black plastic buckets, turned them over, swiped at the bottoms and indicated that she should sit.

Her suit was destined for a trip to the dry cleaners anyway, Claire thought as she perched on the overturned bucket.

Seth hunched forward, leaning his forearms on his knees. "What we'd planned to do was to buy some eggs and some chicks and get started. It'd take a couple of years for us to convert our ranches anyway, and the least expensive way into ostrich farming is buying chicks and fertilized eggs. Beau offered to have the first incubators in his barn. Bellingham is the smallest ranch, but it's central to all of us."

"But what would he have lived on?" Claire asked. "If he didn't have any animals and was just raising chicks, then how could he have supported himself?"

"That's why we formed the partnership," Seth answered. "We'd continue scaling down our cattle and crops and pool a percentage of the profits and compensate Beau from that."

"Sounds reasonable."

"Well, it didn't to your cousins, and they managed to slow things down some."

"I'm sorry," Claire apologized, feeling that it was called for, though she'd had nothing to do with the situation.

Seth shrugged. "Those are the breaks. The thing is, we're moving forward now. We bought the incubators, Beau built this room and we contracted to buy chicks and eggs from a breeder. We were looking around for some immatures—"

"What are those, ostrich teenagers?" Claire teased.

"Yeah."

She'd meant it as a joke, but Seth had answered her seriously. Claire got the idea that ostriches and their potential as livestock were Seth's passions. He gestured with his hands as he talked, looking her straight in the eye as he tried to convince her that he and the other ranchers, including her grandfather, were onto something.

Unfortunately, Claire found herself watching him instead of listening to him. His face was more animated than she'd seen it, and his rich bass voice vibrated through her.

She could see why the other ranchers had chosen him as their spokesman. He was a man's man, decisive and direct. There was meat behind his words, not soufflé.

"Am I boring you?"

Caught daydreaming, Claire's face flamed. "No, but I was thinking."

"About?"

As if she'd tell him the whole truth. "If Bellingham is so crucial to the success of your venture, why didn't Beau just leave the ranch to the partnership? Or to you?"

Seth nodded, as if acknowledging the validity of her question. "From being around you the last couple of days, I've learned that you're a very determined woman. You've got a clear notion of what you want to accomplish in your life and you're setting about doing it. You also know right from wrong and you have a sense of pride and responsibility." He touched the brim of his hat. "I'm pleased to know you."

"You are?"

"Yes, ma'am."

Claire felt a silly grin spread across her face along with a little leftover blush. Pleased and embarrassed, she looked away from the increasingly attractive Seth and stared at the dirt floor.

Where had all her sophistication gone? She'd been flattered before, though perhaps not complimented on those qualities. That must be the reason she felt like a young girl finally noticed by the most popular boy in school.

Get over it, Claire. Seth was an intelligent man. When he saw how his compliments affected her, he'd press his advantage. If she didn't watch out, she'd find herself stuck out here playing mother hen to a flock of ostrich chicks. "Uh, thanks, but that doesn't explain about the ranch."

"I believe that Beau wanted to leave you something, something that would help you get to Paris, maybe. But right now, there isn't much but potential."

People generally used those terms when they were out of money. "What does that mean?"

Seth indicated the room they were sitting in. "All this took a hunk of cash," he said, confirming her suspicions. "It's an investment that won't pay off for a couple of years—or wasn't going to. But that's changed. I told you about the wet spring? Well, a fella down Fredericksburg way wants out of the business. His land keeps flooding and the ostriches get all stressed and won't eat or lay. They don't like wet."

"So you're buying his birds."

"Yes." Seth nodded. "He's got proven breeding pairs he agreed to sell us. Breeders just don't come on the market all that often, and they cost the earth, but we felt that getting up and running two years sooner than we'd expected would be worth it."

Claire's eyes narrowed. "Just how expensive is a breeding pair?"

Seth named a figure that would buy a small Manhattan apartment. It took Claire's breath away. "For *two* birds?"

"They can make you that much in a season. And people are lining up to buy them. That's where we were when Beau died."

"And I've been holding things up, right?"

"It's not your fault. I figure if Beau had left me the ranch, your cousins—and you, for all I know—would have contested the will and tied everything up. Not only would we lose that breeding pair, we'd miss the whole season. Some of the men are hanging on by their fingernails now. They've invested all their cash."

"I see." Unfortunately, she didn't like what she saw.

Seth continued, "If you sold the ranch, none of us could afford to buy it now. Besides, the ranch might not sell for a spell, and the new owners might not want anything to do with the ostrich business."

"No birds, no season." Claire was beginning to understand just what was at stake.

"Right."

"But I don't understand why I couldn't have hired somebody to work the ranch and go along with your plans."

"Have you got that kind of money?"

"Well . . . no, but I could have offered a share in the partnership or something." Claire stood and paced. "*Something* could have been worked out."

Seth sighed, his eyes closed. "I don't know what Beau was thinking, except he probably figured on being around a lot longer."

Claire stopped pacing a little way from Seth. "Had he been sick?"

"Nope. He never complained, never mentioned any pain. Just had a heart attack one night and didn't wake up."

Hugging herself, Claire faced Seth. "And why Texas A&M University?"

"If your cousins contested that, they'd have a costly fight against a battery of lawyers. Besides, A&M

would probably be a silent partner for awhile." He rubbed his temples. "But I'm hoping it doesn't come to that."

"You know, this is making a lot of sense for something that shouldn't make any sense."

"It does." His voice was earnest. "Bellingham isn't worth much now, but in a couple of years—"

"A *couple*?"

"Okay, okay." Seth held his hands palms outward. "Here's my offer. I can't buy Bellingham now, not and buy the breeders, too. If you stay here for a year and just make sure the partnership gets going, we'll buy you out. I don't know how much living in Paris costs these days, but you ought to be able to hold out for a good while on the profits."

It sounded good. Too good. "And if I say no?"

Seth's expression turned bleak. "During the nine months you have to decide, everything will be in limbo. The five of us will carry on, but—" he indicated the barn "—we'll have to build another hatchery and lose the breeders. The whole operation will be delayed." He looked at her. "A couple of the guys will go belly up. We may *all* go belly up."

"Stop it!" Claire raked her fingers through her hair. "You're trying to make it seem like everything is up to me!"

Seth stood and approached her. "Not everything."

But Claire didn't believe him. "You just told me people will lose their homes if I don't stay here!" She collapsed onto the bucket and buried her face in her hands.

Seth didn't say anything. He didn't have to.

Thoughts spun through her mind. She was trapped. "But I don't *want* the responsibility. I know why Beau didn't tell me—he *knew* I'd say no!"

"Don't say no." Seth knelt in front of her.

"Even if I stay, I wouldn't know what to do—"

"I'll help you." His voice was calm and steady, a counterpoint to her rising panic.

She raised her head. "But my work! My job—my apartment. Do you know how hard it is to find an apartment in New York?" she wailed.

"But you're going to Paris," he crooned. "You won't need your apartment." Seth took hold of her arms just below her shoulders. "Claire—look at me." He gripped her arms tighter. "I can make this work. I *will* make it work."

She calmed down as she met his steady, determined gaze.

It was hypnotic, that gaze.

"You do this for me—for the partnership—and I'll see that you get to Paris," he vowed.

Looking at his face, level with hers, Claire almost believed him. "You can't make promises like that."

"Yes, I can, because I *know* this is going to work. We're asking a lot of you, don't think we don't know it."

He was convincing, she'd give him that. For the first time, Claire actually considered what it would mean to stay. "I... I can't just stop working on my designs. I'd lose my clientele."

"Work on them here," Seth said promptly.

"But the eggs and chicks?"

"We'll take care of them."

She bit the inside of her cheek. "I'd have to give up my job."

"Can't help that, but we'd support you the same way we were going to support Beau." He released her arms. "You won't starve. Besides, think of the rent money you'll save."

He had a point. She'd have no income, but no outgo, either. It might work.

Heaven help her, she was actually considering it.

They didn't expect her to do anything, just keep the vultures away. She could work on her designs, and at the end of the year, she'd have money for Paris.

If she didn't stay, she'd be responsible for turning people out of their homes.

What choice did she have, really?

"Claire?" Seth gazed intently at her. "Will you stay?"

Sighing, she gazed around the hatchery, then at the brown-eyed rancher who'd turned her world upside-down.

"Yes," she said. "I can't believe it, but I'm going to stay."

CHAPTER FOUR

SETH nodded as if he'd anticipated her capitulation all along. "Good."

That was it? Just good? Apparently so, Claire decided as Seth stood and offered her a hand.

She half-expected, hoped, really, that he'd throw his hat in the air and whoop with joy, then swing her around like cowboys always did in the movies. After all, she'd saved the ranch, hadn't she? She was a heroine.

Seth was no celluloid cowboy, that was for sure.

"I'll tell the others and call about that breeding pair. We're already a couple of months into the laying season and don't want to waste any more time." As he spoke, Seth was striding across the graveled yard. Claire supposed she was to follow along like a good girl.

She followed, but at her own pace. Moments ago, he'd had her believing she was the most important person in the ostrich project. People's futures hung on her decision. She'd only just agreed to stay, and already Seth was taking her for granted.

Claire didn't like being ignored. She was dedicating a year of her life to help these people. A year!

She stopped walking as the enormity of her decision sank in. Seth had blithely told her she could work on her designs during her year at the ranch, but he had no idea what was involved. How could he?

How could he know that the streets of New York inspired many of Claire's ideas? Or that she'd return from a trip to the fabric markets with swatches that fueled her latest creations? She *needed* New York for inspiration and for contacts.

What about her job with Audrey? Claire knew Audrey could easily find another salesclerk, but the job was Claire's chance to interact with the women she designed for. She needed their feedback. How else could she have learned that transparent neon vinyl fabric fogged up when it was worn?

Without her job at Audrey's, Claire was out of the loop. By the time a trend made it here, to the hinterlands, it would be passé. And so would she.

Her career was doomed. She'd have to start all over again, maybe even take another name.

Seth had reached the porch steps before noticing she wasn't behind him. "You all right?" he called.

"No, I'm not all right!" she yelled back.

"What's wrong?" He started toward her in an easy loping stride.

"I'm having second thoughts, I'm wondering if I've just committed career suicide, and I'm mourning my ruined boots!"

"What's happened to your boots?" Seth asked when he reached her.

"Just look."

He squatted to examine them. In typically male fashion, he disregarded her emotional turmoil, focusing on what he considered most important. Boots.

"The gravel chewed off the suede," she complained, grabbing his shoulder while she lifted one boot so he could see the gouges along the heel.

"They're not made to hold up to rough walking," Seth commented, rubbing at the streaks.

"I wasn't planning to wear them for hiking," Claire informed him, conscious of his muscles bunching under her hands. From the back of her mind came the niggling thought that if Seth hadn't been such an attractive man, he might have had a more difficult time convincing her to remain at Bellingham.

Seth squinted at her. "What were you going to do when it rained or snowed in New York?"

"Not wear them," she replied as he stood.

"They aren't very practical, then, are they?"

"Of course they are, they're black." Or they were.

Out of the corner of her eye, she saw him shake his head. She hadn't expected him to understand. Even so, doubts began to assail her. She was going to get as banged up living on the ranch as her boots were now.

They set off toward the house. "Seth, I'm not sure me living here will work." Claire wasn't going to go back on her word, but he seemed to minimize the problems she was likely to encounter.

"Because you ruined your boots?" He matched her pace this time.

Claire waved her hand. "Because I'm not cut out for this life. I'm like the suede—soft and impractical. The pioneer life isn't for me."

"Pioneer!" Seth chuckled, then his laughter grew. "Heck fire, ma'am, we got indoor plumbin' and everythin'."

Claire was not amused. "I was trying to express my doubts and misgivings to you and you're laughing at me."

He sobered as they reached the steps. "I wasn't laughing at you—well, not much, anyway." Another chuckle escaped him, quickly squelched when he met her infuriated gaze. "It's just that you New Yorkers always think we live in the Dark Ages. You'll find that we don't."

"Ha! Depends on your definition." Claire eyed him a moment before climbing the steps. "I remember what it was like living here that summer."

"Claire, wait up." Seth joined her at the top of the stairs. "It's not going to be as bad as you're making it out to be."

"No? I'm going to be stuck here with just a bunch of birds for company. Sounds pretty bad to me."

"Claire?"

"What?"

As she watched, a slow smile spread across his face, and his eyes softened. "Thanks."

Claire carried the memory of the warm approval in that smile and her response to it with her as she prepared to move to Bellingham.

She winced for her apartment, snapped up within hours, and the fact that Audrey didn't seem at all upset by Claire's leaving. In fact, Claire met her replacement before she left New York.

One of the last things she did before flying to Texas was to visit her favorite wholesale fabric importer and splurge on three bolts of coordinating fabric.

She may have to endure Bellingham, but she most certainly did *not* have to endure that hideous olive, tan and yellow upholstery.

She'd hoped Seth would meet her at the airport, and was disappointed that he'd sent Pete's wife, the woman who'd been feeding Claire's chickens, to drive her to Bellingham. By the time they pulled onto the ranch's roadway, Claire had given Mrs. Stevens the chickens in exchange for eggs whenever Claire wanted them. Each woman thought she'd made a terrific bargain.

Making Mrs. Stevens's acquaintance almost made up for the fact that Seth had palmed Claire off on someone else.

She'd been looking forward to seeing him again. That smile on the porch had been full of promise. For the first time, she thought he was seeing her as someone other than Beau's granddaughter or the woman who could foil his ostrich plans. He was seeing her as a person. As a woman—as an *attractive* woman, perhaps, if Claire hadn't misread the expression in his eyes.

They could indulge in a light flirtation over the next year, she thought. Naturally, they both knew nothing serious could come of it, since if all went well she'd be on her way to Paris this time next year.

April in Paris. Claire sighed. She'd hold onto that thought.

In the meantime, she'd explore *why* cowboys held such appeal. It would be fun, she thought, smiling as Mrs. Stevens turned into the Bellingham entrance.

Seth and the others had been busy during the week Claire had been away.

A new shed stood near the hatchery. Metal fencing staked out a modest square and separated it from the field alongside. In the big field, men were laying out long runs.

Ranch hands wandered all over the place, and a truck dumped a load of sand in the new fenced area.

From the looks of the hills of sand, this wasn't the first truckload.

What were they going to use all that sand for?

"Looks different, doesn't it?" Pete's wife backed her pickup truck close to the ranch house.

"Yes." Claire could hardly believe the changes. "Isn't it a little soon to be putting up all that fencing?"

"Well—" Mrs. Stevens hedged. "Seth can tell you what everything's for. The rest of us just go along with him."

Claire was beginning to see that she wasn't the only one caught up in Seth's vision.

"When do you expect the rest of your things?" Mrs. Stevens asked as she turned off the engine.

"By the end of the week, though I don't have all that much." Claire got out of the pickup truck, walked around to the bed and patted the largest box. "As long as I've got my sewing machine, I'll keep busy."

"You enjoy sewing?" Mrs. Stevens asked her, a delighted expression on her face.

"I design clothes," Claire answered, though she was certain that everyone already knew all about her. She'd no doubt been the object of the county gossips for weeks. "And until I get so famous I can hire someone else to do it, I still sew all my designs myself."

"We must have you to our sewing circle, then," Mrs. Stevens pronounced.

"That sounds nice. Perhaps sometime when I'm not so pressured with my work," she said. The last thing she needed was more sewing.

"I see." Mrs. Stevens's smile faded. She lowered the back of the pickup so Claire could unload her luggage. "Pete!" she called, cupping her hands around her mouth. "You and some of the boys come help unload Claire's things."

Claire hoped one of the "boys" would be Seth. He knew she was to arrive today—at least he could be here to welcome her. She'd dressed carefully this time, in her new black jeans and a pair of ankle boots that had already seen two winters in New York. She was making an effort to fit in and wanted him to see. But he wasn't among the three men who approached them, and Claire wasn't going to ask about him.

"Howdy, Claire," Pete hailed her. "You ready to get settled in?"

"I sure am," she answered. "What's going on over there?"

Pete looked toward the barn before climbing into the pickup bed. "We're preparing the pens for the ostriches."

Claire lifted her arms to accept one of her suitcases. "But I thought there were just going to be eggs and chicks here at Bellingham."

Pete gestured for one of the other men to help him with Claire's sewing machine. "That's what we thought, but you don't have dogs."

Of course. This explanation made perfect sense.

Claire was about to ask what the old rancher meant when a vehicle turned in at the Bellingham gate. Seth's Jeep Cherokee.

It's about time, she thought, deliberately glancing away. She wasn't about to be caught mooning over the handsome rancher.

"Hey, there's Seth." Pete waved and grinned, giving Claire an excuse to watch Seth's approach.

The closer he got, the faster her heart beat. They'd only spoken once on the telephone while she was gone, when he'd asked her if she'd like him to hire someone to clean the house before she moved in. Having just finished scrubbing her own apartment, Claire had agreed.

He'd sounded cordial but not especially warm on the telephone. Then when he hadn't met her at the airport, Claire thought he might be distancing himself, so she didn't know what to expect when Seth drove into the ranch yard.

"You made it," he said with an easy smile, and slammed the door of the Cherokee.

"Yeah," Claire said, as tongue-tied as a schoolgirl.

He looked good. Very cowboyish in his jeans and Western shirt. She saw him glance at her feet, then chuckle. "We'll make a cowgirl out of you yet."

Had he expected her to make the same mistake she'd made last week? Those boots and the clothes she'd brought had stayed here so she could fill her suitcases with the rest of her wardrobe. She may be a city girl at heart, but that didn't mean she couldn't go native if she had to. After all, Seth had worn city dress when he'd visited New York.

After nodding greetings to the men and Mrs. Stevens, he turned to Claire. "There's no turning back now, is there?"

"You mean I had an option?"

He laughed. "*You* did. We didn't."

Their gazes held for a moment, and Claire saw the relief in his eyes.

"You thought I wouldn't come after all?"

Shrugging, he opened the back of his Jeep. "Once you got back to New York, there was always the chance you'd change your mind."

Claire abandoned her suitcase and wandered over to him. "You'd just drag me back."

"Probably," he agreed with a casual matter-of-factness. "Here, carry this." He handed her a box.

Claire peered inside. "Food?"

Seth grabbed two sacks. "I figured you wouldn't feel like driving into Royerville today."

Claire was touched, more so at his next words.

"My mother sent over a casserole for you."

"She did?" This was a good sign, Claire thought, and wondered what Seth had told his mother about her. "That was very thoughtful of her. My cooking skills are a little rusty."

"Are you saying you can't cook?" Seth fell into step next to her.

"No, I suppose I can cook. But living alone, I just ate out a lot or picked up something from the deli." She hoped he realized she was telling him that there hadn't been anyone special in the life she'd left behind. Not that he'd asked.

"Claire?" Mrs. Stevens met them at the porch. "Where do you want your sewing machine?"

"Put it by the front window for now," she answered. "The light is best there."

Feeling cheered, Claire led the way to the kitchen and set her box on the counter. This wouldn't be so bad. With everyone pitching in to help, she'd be unpacked and working again soon.

"You've got a deep freeze, which should be fairly well stocked. Beau laid in a side of beef last winter." Seth eased the sacks down next to her box. "It's in the pantry, there." He pointed to a door.

Claire opened the pantry to find mostly cans of soup and beans, crackers and several jars of tomatoes and some green vegetables. Probably gifts from neighboring ranch wives, she surmised.

A hulking white freezer hummed loudly. "This thing looks like it's fifty years old."

"Might be," Seth agreed. "Your grandmother probably kept it full."

Claire stared at the old machine. "Did you know my grandmother?" she asked.

"No," Seth said gently.

"Neither did I." Claire moved the cans to one side to sort through later. "She died before I was born."

"I would have been just a little kid, then."

Claire looked around. "You know, I'm beginning to think that my grandfather didn't change a thing here in the last thirty years."

She was referring to the decor, but Seth took it in a larger sense. "Things don't change much around here," he said, digging in the sacks and withdrawing the food that needed refrigeration. "That's why it was so hard to commit to the ostriches."

"Speaking of," Claire said, "what is going on with all the sand and fences?"

"Well...we had a little change of plan."

"What do you mean?" she asked sharply.

"We hadn't figured on the dogs. Here." He tossed her a head of lettuce.

"Dogs?"

"Hyenas and jackals are natural predators of ostriches. The birds look at a dog and they think, 'Danger, there's a weird-looking hyena.'"

Claire laughed.

"They look at a horse and they see a zebra." He grinned. "But you should've seen the horses when they first laid eyes on those eight-foot birds."

"Seth, are you telling me the ostriches are going to stay here?" That hadn't been their agreement. If he was changing things already, what else would he change?

"We think it would be best," he said with a sidelong glance. "We just got the breeding pair and the hen hasn't laid since she was moved. She's stressed."

"I know exactly how she feels," Claire retorted.

"Ruben keeps dogs, and they've been yapping at the birds night and day."

"So I get the ostriches."

"It makes sense. Now we don't have to move the eggs so far. You've got the incubators right here."

"But—"

"Don't worry, Claire. All it'll mean to you is that you'll have to put up with seeing me more often."

Oh. Well, then. She'd just have to make the sacrifice. "Uh, how many birds?"

A smile lit Seth's face. "The two breeders I told you about earlier, and then we ran into a bit of luck. We've got a lead on some twenty-month-old birds, as well. They may or may not lay this season."

"Claire? Seth? Y'all in here?" Pete and his wife came in. "We're going to head on back to our place now. Anything you need, Claire?"

She looked around at the abundance of food. "I'm not going to starve anytime soon, thanks to Seth."

"We're none of us going to starve, thanks to Seth." Mrs. Stevens beamed at him.

"Don't go making me out to be a hero," he protested. "It's going to be a lot of work."

From the looks on their faces, Claire knew that his protests had fallen on deaf ears. Pete and his wife clearly worshiped Seth.

The ranchers' situation must be grim, Claire realized. As Seth walked the Stevenses to the door and said goodbye, Claire thought about the kind of man who could convince an entire community to change the way things had been done for generations. The ostriches were a gamble, and if they failed, Seth would be the sort of man who held himself responsible. He'd probably work the rest of his life trying to pay everyone back, too.

After they left, Claire and Seth finished putting away the groceries.

"I need to check on things down at the barn," he said.

And then he'd leave. Claire didn't want him to leave yet. She wanted to learn more about the man who could inspire such respect. "After you finish at the barn, why don't you come back here and share your mother's casserole with me?" She sounded a little too breathless and eager.

He hesitated, and Claire chastised herself. She was being too obvious. She was mistaking neighborly kindness for something else. All he'd done was smile at her, and she was reading all sorts of hidden meanings into his actions.

She needed to get a grip on her runaway emotions. She barely knew the man. Of course, she hoped to change that, but maybe she was being too forward. Maybe women around here didn't issue dinner invitations to men.

Or maybe he had a girlfriend.

Or maybe—

"Thanks, Claire. I'd like that." He smiled again.

Gosh, he had a great smile. Claire gave a tiny sigh.

"Well, I'd better—"

"I should—"

They both spoke at the same time, then broke off with embarrassed laughs.

Seth backed out the door, and Claire wanted to sink into a hole.

She was acting like a student with a crush on her teacher.

Slipping the casserole into the huge old oven, Claire gave herself a stern lecture. Embarrassing Seth by coming on too strong would make for a very uncomfortable year.

She could see right now that even a light flirtation was out of the question. Seth wasn't the light flirtation type. He had a ranch to run, not a nine-to-five job that left his evenings free. She'd better cool it, or at least let him take the lead. Now all she had to do was get him to lead.

Claire spent the next hour busier than she expected to be. Checking the cabinets, she discovered a mismatched collection of cracked and chipped plates and cups. She swore there weren't two matching glasses to be found.

This was awful. Her dishes were being shipped with the rest of her things, or she would have used them.

At least she could do something about the table, but though she searched, she couldn't find a tablecloth or napkins.

Eventually, Claire took the crocheted doilies from the tops of the bureaus in her grandfather's room and the room she used. There were paper napkins in the cabinet above the refrigerator, which she supposed would have to do.

She looked outside the back door of the kitchen, hoping to find some flowers. No flowers, but she did find a vegetable garden that her grandfather had planted before he died. Weeds sprouted among the plants. Fresh vegetables, Claire thought, intrigued, but having no idea what was growing. Maybe Seth could identify the plants for her.

A few bluebonnets and wildflowers dotted the unkempt backyard. Claire picked a bunch and set them on the table in one of the white cracked mugs. Standing back, she admired the effect. Casual and country. Not bad, if she kept the lights low.

Now for dinner. Claire opened the oven door and was assailed by a scorched smell. Great. What would Seth think when he found that she'd burned his mother's casserole? Where were the oven mitts?

In a drawer next to the oven, fortunately. Removing the baking dish, Claire peeled off the aluminum foil and was relieved to see that just the cheese around the edges was burned.

What else to serve?

Seth arrived while she was in the pantry. "I see things are coming along," he said, washing his hands.

"Yes, but dinner's not quite ready yet." Claire was uncomfortably aware that she should have been cooking the food instead of worrying about the appearance of the table.

She emerged from the pantry to find Seth peering under the foil. "King Ranch Chicken. One of my favorites."

"I hope you like it crispy around the edges." She smiled tightly. "I thought we'd have this with it." She held up one of the green vegetable jars and searched for a pot.

"Uh, Claire?"

"Yes?" She'd found a battered saucepan and was considering whether or not to wash it first.

"I believe that's pickled okra. You don't want to cook it."

Claire stared at the jar. She'd thought it contained string beans. Really fat string beans. "You thought I was going to cook the okra?" She laughed. *What in the heck was okra*? "The pot's for...for potatoes."

"You think we'll need them?" He looked doubtful. "They'll take a while to boil."

"Oh, no," Claire reassured him, glad not to appear a total culinary incompetent. "They just take eight minutes in the microwave."

Seth's gaze flicked around the kitchen. "Microwave?"

Claire closed her eyes. "I don't have a microwave, do I?"

"Not unless you brought one with you."

"Scratch the potatoes, then," she said, her voice too bright.

With a sense of desperation, she yanked open the refrigerator, thankful to see the head of lettuce. "Salad. We'll have salad."

Seth didn't say much as she threw together the salad. She wished he'd wait in the other room, but he just watched her, offering innocuous comments about the ranching families living around her.

Claire wasn't paying attention. The kitchen was as foreign to her as ranch life, and now Seth knew it. Her lack of culinary expertise had never bothered her before. What was it about Seth that prompted this uncharacteristic foray into domesticity?

They sat down to a dinner of burned casserole, salad and pickled okra.

"This'll be Ruben's wife's okra," Seth offered when Claire let the conversation lag.

That was something else Claire noticed. Women here were So-and-so's wife. She supposed that made her Beau's granddaughter. "Oh?" she said, eyeing the okra she'd been afraid to eat.

"Might be kind of spicy. Beau loved it."

Now she had to eat it. Smiling gamely, Claire speared a green pod with her fork and bit off a small piece.

Liquid fire engulfed her tongue and lips. She blinked away tears. "I see what you mean." She drank her entire glass of water, but it didn't help.

Before she finished, Seth was at the refrigerator, pouring her a glass of milk. "Try this."

Claire would have tried anything at this point. The milk did help, though. "Thanks."

The casserole had been spicy, too. It was a wonder these people had any living taste buds. Claire finished her salad and called it a meal.

"Would you like some coffee?" she offered.

Smiling his refusal, Seth rose. "I need to be getting back to my place. The days start early." He carried his plate to the sink.

"Thanks for keeping me company on my first evening." Claire suspected he had much to do and was touched that he'd spent the extra time with her. "You go on. I'll take care of the dishes," she said when Seth started to rinse off his plate.

He didn't argue with her. "I'll check back with you tomorrow, then." As he prepared to leave, he stopped. "I forgot. I've got something for you."

He disappeared into the other room, returning with a box. "Housewarming present."

"For me?" This almost made up for the dinner disaster.

She pulled off the top and stared at a familiar pair of black boots. "These look just like mine. In fact—" she looked at him "—they are mine, aren't they?"

"Take a look." Seth pulled one out.

Claire did, and saw a beautiful, gouge-free suede boot. "You had them repaired!" She examined the heels. "The suede matches perfectly."

"Of course." Seth grinned. "Don't forget you're living in Texas now. We aren't about to be stumped by a pair of New York boots."

CHAPTER FIVE

FORGET she was living in Texas? Not likely.

She was stranded here. If the past few days were a sample of how her year would go, Claire honestly didn't know if she'd be able to stick it out.

After the welcoming flurry that first day, she was pretty much ignored by the ranch personnel—and by Seth.

When she saw him working with the men at the barn, Claire would go outside, but after a couple of forays, it was obvious that she was in the way.

"Did you need something?" he'd asked her once, clearly harried. "If not, I'm kinda busy here." The men with him watched her, their faces carefully expressionless. It gave her the creeps.

"No, I'm busy, too," she'd answered, backing up as she spoke. "Just thought I'd say hello."

He nodded and everyone turned away from her.

Well, pardon me for being civil, she'd thought, walking back to the ranch house. After that, she'd waited for him to stop by the ranch house, but he hadn't.

And neither had anyone else.

Then there were the ostriches. No one had told her when they were to arrive. She just happened to look outside one morning when a horse trailer pulled into the gravel drive and continued on to the newly fenced area around the barn. Seth yanked open the door, and two huge birds scuttled into their new home. Seth and the men lined up at the fence and watched for a long time. Claire expected him to invite her to take a look, or at least call her attention to the ostriches, though they were hard to ignore.

But he hadn't. It was almost as if he was avoiding her.

Claire knew he was busy, so she tried not to take her snubbing personally, but it was hard. She was trying to stay out of the way and obviously succeeding all too well.

Seth hadn't called or visited her once since the dinner she fixed—or attempted to fix. She'd long since washed his mother's casserole dish and wanted to return it, but had no way of getting to the Montgomery Rose except on foot.

Her grandfather's one remaining horse was boarded at somebody's ranch, she couldn't remember whose. Of course, she hadn't ridden a horse since her summer here. Did she even remember how to saddle one? Probably not.

There was always the truck. An ancient red pickup truck was parked under a wooden awning out back. Assorted rusting pieces of machinery kept it company. The whole area was home to a number of small scurrying creatures Claire chose not to disturb.

Assuming she had the keys, which she didn't, and assuming the truck would even start, which she doubted, Claire didn't know how to drive. She was completely dependent on her neighbors for transportation, and they'd been none too neighborly.

In fact, Claire had the distinct impression that the ranchers and their families resented her when she'd expected them to be grateful.

She didn't belong here. What could her grandfather have been thinking? The slim bundle of letters she'd received from him was in with her personal papers, which were in her bedroom, waiting to be unpacked. Claire hadn't had the opportunity to reread them as she'd intended. Now she planned to examine every line, every casual comment for a deeper meaning. Maybe she'd missed something before.

Her mother hadn't known of her grandfather's death, and hadn't cared for her former father-in-law. She was astounded that Claire had even considered living at Bellingham.

"You don't owe those people anything," she'd said, when Claire tried to explain.

But Claire inexplicably *did* feel she owed the ranchers something. Seth had made her feel that way. He'd made her care about the ostrich venture and what it would mean to the ranchers in this area. They wanted to save their ranches and they were willing to gamble to do it. Claire admired that.

Now, watching the activity out by the barn from her front window, Claire pondered how best to approach Seth with her concerns and questions. Thanks to his thoughtfulness with the groceries, she was set for a while, but she was running low on milk and had eaten the entire head of lettuce. She liked salads, but Seth couldn't have known that.

Claire turned away from the window and stared at the mountain of boxes and packing trash in the living room. How was she to dispose of it all? Was there regular trash collection out here in the country?

Sighing, she added that question to the list she'd begun yesterday.

As she wrote, she heard a cheer from the workers outside. Claire ran to the window but couldn't tell what had prompted the celebration, so she decided to investigate. At the last moment, she took her list with her.

The men had disappeared into the ostrich barn by the time Claire reached it. Looking for Seth, she located him next to the incubator, surrounded by the crowd of grinning ranchers. One tinkered with the incubator and the rest encircled a work table.

She stood watching for several moments, but couldn't see past the wall of ranchers. No one noticed her. Drawing a deep breath, she approached Seth and tapped him on the shoulder. "Hi, what's going on?" she asked.

He glanced at her before brushing at a large globe nestled in a padded box. "Phoebe laid an egg."

No, "Howdy, Claire," no smile, no nothing. "Phoebe? Is that the ostrich's name?"

He nodded. "And Phineas is the male."

"Odd names for ostriches," she commented, aware that the other three men had barely acknowledged her presence. She'd seen them around the ranch the past three days, but she didn't know who they were, and no one had introduced her.

"And what do you think are typical ostrich names?" Seth, moving with great care, picked up the egg and transferred it to a scale.

"I'd never really considered it before. I didn't think they had names."

"Yep." He steadied the egg, then removed his hands and squinted at the scale. "Three pounds, nine ounces," he read. "A little on the small side, but we'll take it, right?"

There was murmured agreement among the others. Seth picked up the egg. "Out of the way, Claire. You're standing in front of the incubator."

She stepped back, then had to step back again as she bumped into a table.

"Rotators working?" Seth asked one of the men, then set the egg carefully in one of the holders. "In forty-one to forty-three days, we'll have our first ostrich chick. That's when your work will really start, Claire." He smiled at her.

"I have work now," she said at once. "I'm *very* busy with my designs," she stressed. "Ostrich work isn't part of our agreement." She'd been afraid this very thing would happen. The sooner he understood that she planned to hold him to their deal, the better.

The men all looked at Seth.

"Calm down. It was just a slip of the tongue." Seth's smile faded immediately, and Claire could have kicked herself. "I haven't forgotten our agreement."

Why couldn't she have kept her big mouth shut? She was searching for a way to apologize when one of the men spoke.

"Hey, Seth, shall we go ahead and order another incubator? Now that Phoebe's laying, this sixteen-egg model won't be enough."

Seth stared at the incubator. "I'm thinking we might see if that used fifty-egg model is still available."

They all stared at the metal box. A clear window in front revealed three trays with divided compartments that could each hold an egg. The one egg looked lonely.

"It'll probably cost more than a brand-new sixteen-egg incubator," one man finally commented.

"And we've still got to buy heating pads and flooring," another rancher pointed out.

Claire shifted her weight from one foot to the other. The discussion about egg incubators, scintillating though it might be, did not interest her. She was impatient to talk with Seth alone.

"We don't absolutely have to buy flooring for another six weeks. And wouldn't two new sixteen-egg incubators cost more than the used fifty-egg size?" Seth asked the group. They all frowned and deliberated his question.

Claire wanted to scream. She would've left, except she was afraid she'd never get to talk to Seth, especially since she knew she'd alienated him. "I'd go for the used one," she said into the silence.

Four male heads turned toward her. "I faced the same situation with my sewing machine. It was more than I needed at the time, but I grew into it faster than I'd expected. I never regretted investing more up front, because I saved money and time later." She shrugged. "What happens if you get a good deal on some other ostriches? You'd have to buy another incubator then, anyway. Why not be prepared now?"

The men looked at each other. "Sounds good to me," Seth said with an approving look at Claire.

The others made unintelligible sounds that Claire took for agreement. She hoped she'd made up for her thoughtless remark earlier.

"I'll get right on it then," one of the men said and left, followed shortly by the other.

And at last Claire was alone with Seth. Alone except for Phoebe and Phineas, that is.

Seth wandered over to the sandy, fenced enclosure and stared out at the birds.

Claire followed him. "I've wanted to return your mother's casserole dish," she said as the ostriches peered at them.

"Drop it by whenever you're finished with it."

There was no way to interpret that statement as a desire to see her again, Claire realized, disappointed. She'd really blown it. Whatever small attraction he'd felt for her was gone. Still, a lot could happen in a year. "About how far would you say your ranch house is from here?"

One of the birds approached, then the other.

"About fifteen miles southeast of here as the crow flies."

"Fifteen miles!" So much for an afternoon walk. "And you consider yourself a neighbor?"

He turned his attention from the ostriches and looked at her. "I am. Pete lives even farther away."

Claire was shaken when she realized her neighbors were miles away. "You mean I'm all alone out here?"

"Unless you hire a ranch hand, yes." Seth didn't seem the slightest bit concerned.

"*I* hire one?" she spluttered.

"Well, yes, if you want somebody to live out here. We're taking turns sending over men to work with the ostriches, so there'll usually be people around during the daytime."

Claire felt better. Not much, but a little better.

Phoebe and Phineas reached the fence. Claire backed up. The birds were huge, about eight feet tall, and they had enormous eyes with lovely long eyelashes. And the feathers. Lush black and white on the male, brownish on the female. Claire knew what ostrich feathers wholesaled for in New York. She hadn't used them in her designs, but now...

"See that toe with the claw?" Seth pointed at the ostriches' feet. "If the ostriches get riled, they'll kick. They can kill a man that way."

They were dangerous? "Oh, great! Man-killing birds, and you guys go in there and steal their eggs?"

Seth laughed. "The trick is not to rile them."

"Stealing my eggs would rile me."

The ostriches stared at her. Why her and not Seth? She stepped sideways. Their heads turned in unison. She stepped back toward Seth. The ostriches followed her movements.

"They're staring at me."

"You're a right purty lady."

"Give me a break. Quit talking that way, too."

Seth chuckled. "I don't know, something about you interests them."

She wished she had something that interested *him*. Sighing, she started to reply when one of the birds, moving at lightning speed, stuck its head over the fence and pecked at the side of her face.

Claire yelped and flung herself at Seth. His arms closed around her protectively and he whipped around until his back was to the birds.

"It attacked me!" Claire's heart pounded so hard and so fast she couldn't tell where one beat stopped and the next began. She clung to Seth, gulping air.

"It's okay," he said, murmuring soothingly, his hands stroking her back.

Gradually Claire calmed down enough to feel embarrassed for overreacting.

But not embarrassed enough to pull away.

As she got over her initial start, she became aware of Seth, of his strong arms and solid chest. The leathery outdoors smell she'd come to associate with him mingled with a faint scent she recognized as the starch in his shirt.

He moved his hand up her back and caressed her hair, still murmuring as though she were a skittish colt.

Claire shivered. She wanted to stay in his arms. As improbable as it was to her, being held by Seth felt right.

They were from two different worlds, and she would only be a part of his world for a year, but right now, Claire didn't think of that. She thought only of how safe he made her feel. Protected and feminine. *Domestic*, even. These were alien feelings to her, and she wanted time to sort them out.

But not until she absolutely had to leave his arms.

"You okay, now?" he asked after several seconds.

Nodding, Claire released her death grip on him. "I feel embarrassed for overreacting like that." *But I don't regret a moment of it.*

"You were startled. It's understandable when you aren't used to animals." He held her at arm's length. "Now let's see what old Phineas wanted." His gaze swept over her. "Ah, your earrings."

Claire wore the Austrian crystal ones from Audrey's shop. "Why does he want earrings? He doesn't have any ears."

Grinning, Seth explained, "Ostriches like bright, shiny things. You've got to watch it. They'll go after anything, I've heard." He gently touched her earlobe, sending a giant spark zinging down the side of her neck. "No damage. He could have torn your earlobe."

"Gee." Claire brought her hand to her ear and glared at Phineas. "At least you've got good taste."

Laughing, Seth draped an arm around her shoulder and started walking in the direction of his truck, a vehicle Claire hadn't seen him drive before. "Time for me to get going. I'll try to get back here later on, but I might not make it."

He was coming back! He was coming back! She hoped he was over his irritation with her. She'd better play it cool. "That reminds me, I've got some questions for you."

Seth looked at his watch. "Better make them quick."

His impatience annoyed Claire, but she tried not to show it. She dug in the pocket of her jeans for her list. "When is the trash pickup around here?"

He looked blank.

"I've got all my moving boxes and packing material piled in the living room," she explained.

"And you want to throw good boxes away? What are you going to use when you move to Paris?"

"I..." Claire had assumed that she'd buy more. "They're taking up so much room."

"So break them down and store them flat."

Obviously, one didn't waste boxes on the ranch. "I'll do that." Maybe. "I suppose I'm not used to having any storage space after living in an apartment for so long. But, when I do have trash, when is the pickup?"

"Whenever you want. We do our own hauling around here."

Claire bit her lip. "And where do we haul it?"

"The dump. You want directions?"

"Is it far away?"

"I suppose you'd think so, but you probably won't be going out there more than once a month or so," he informed her.

"Once a month?" Lovely. "The garbage will smell."

"Smell?" He looked at her accusingly. "You aren't putting your kitchen scraps in the trash are you?"

"I wrap them first."

Seth shook his head. "That's what the compost heap is for. You put your scraps out there and they'll decompose into rich dirt that you'll use in your vegetable garden."

Claire heard *dirt and vegetable garden*. She'd ignored the vegetable garden since discovering it the day she'd arrived. "Oh."

"Anything else?"

"Yes, wait a minute and I'll get your mother's dish so you can take it with you." Claire ran into the house and got the dish. By the time she made it outside, Seth was already sitting in his truck.

Claire passed the dish in through the window. "And also, could you let me know the next time you're planning a trip to the grocery store? I'd appreciate a ride."

He smiled as he started the motor. "I don't usually do the grocery shopping, but I'll let you know next time I plan a trip into town. I don't know when that'll be, though."

Great. How long would she have to wait for lettuce?

"Why the long face? You don't have to wait on me. Or isn't Beau's truck working?"

"I don't know." Claire was getting frustrated. "It wouldn't matter if it did because I don't know how to drive."

He stared at her, then cut the engine. "You don't know how to drive a stick shift, or you don't know how to drive, period?"

"I don't know how to drive, period."

"Anything?"

She shook her head. "I never needed to."

Emotions flitted across his face as he grappled with this new information. "Why didn't you say something?" he asked at last.

He looked so put out that Claire got angry, too. "And just when would I have said anything? I've been here nearly a week, and other than your mother sending her casserole, nobody has called or visited or paid me any attention at all! If I hadn't come out to the barn today, you would've left just like you have all the other days!"

"I didn't want to bother you at your... work," he said with just the slightest hesitation.

But Claire heard it. He was sneering at her. All the resentment that had been building and she'd been denying boiled out. "You begged me to disrupt my entire life for you, and once you got your way, you forgot all about me! I'm all alone out here! I could starve or get sick or something and you wouldn't even know it!"

Then she said something she knew she shouldn't. "Is that what happened to my grandfather? You convinced him to turn his ranch over to the ostriches and then you ignored him, too?"

Seth blanched, then was out of the truck like a shot. He gripped her shoulders. "Don't you accuse me of neglecting *your* grandfather! You, who stand to benefit from all his hard work and never bothered to come and see him."

"Beau never came to see me, either!"

"Maybe he didn't think he'd be welcome."

"Or maybe he just hated New York."

"The way you hate the ranch?" His eyes blazed into hers.

Claire looked away.

"Oh, yes." Seth released her, though she could still feel the force of his grip. "You've made it plain that you want nothing to do with ranch life or the ostriches. You have reminded me and anybody who'll listen at every opportunity. You don't even want to try to fit in. You're here for what you can get, and when you've got it, you're gone."

"There wouldn't be anything to get if it weren't for me!" she lashed out. "You'd all be homeless. Only you seem to have forgotten that, haven't you?"

Seth visibly withdrew. "I'm sorry," he apologized formally.

His brown eyes were hard. Claire preferred him yelling at her.

"We're all aware that it's in our best interest to keep you happy here."

"I wasn't threatening you," Claire protested.

Seth got into the pick up. "Really?"

"No! I wouldn't do that."

But he didn't believe her, she could tell by his face.

"I've got to leave. I'll see about finding someone who can spare the time to teach you how to drive," he said, and put the truck into reverse. He backed it up, then shifted gears. With a curt nod to her, he drove away, leaving her standing in the gravel drive.

It was hard to believe that the kind man who comforted her when Phineas scared her was the same man who'd just left her.

Their argument had erupted out of nowhere. It couldn't have been just because she didn't know how to drive. Granted, she was out of line to accuse him of neglecting her grandfather. Beau Bellingham wasn't his responsibility, but Claire was, in a way. She should have been more diplomatic about expressing her resentment at being ignored.

As she climbed the porch steps, which still sagged and still were a safety hazard, she tried to remember what he'd said in response. Something about Claire benefiting from her grandfather's work without doing any herself.

That's gratitude for you, she thought and slammed the screen door to blow off steam. And her relationship with her grandfather was none of his business.

Claire flopped onto the hideous tan and olive couch. The light faded, but she didn't turn on the lamps. The room looked better in the dark.

Seth's remark about her not trying to fit in was harder to defend. It bothered her that Seth thought she was threatening him with leaving before the year was up. She'd only just arrived!

Perhaps she should make the first effort in inviting Pete's wife and some of the other ranch wives over for coffee. Isn't that what was done? Claire had a feeling that a cocktail party wasn't the way to go. And with coffee, she could get away with serving a cake or cookies. She didn't trust herself to cook a complete meal yet.

So she'd invite them for coffee. That's what she'd do. They'd probably been gossiping about her, and the only way to counter that was to invite them over so they could meet her. She'd be charming and gracious and maybe explain a little of her work. When they saw that she wasn't just lazing about, they'd be more understanding.

She flipped on the lamp and gazed around the room. The three bolts of fabric stood in the corner, and Claire smiled. Time to decorate. Recovering the furniture and putting up new curtains would send a message to the ranching community that Claire Bellingham was staying.

For a year, anyway.

CHAPTER SIX

A SCREECHING groan accompanied Claire's attempts to drive the pickup truck from its spot under the awning.

Seth winced. "Do you think you could let the clutch out easier?"

"Any easier and the motor will die again." The motor died anyway. Claire banged on the wheel in frustration.

"Try keeping your foot on the gas," Seth offered, and rubbed at a spot between his eyebrows.

Her foot *was* on the gas. In fact, it was pressed all the way to the floorboard. The starter motor ground in ever slowing waves until she gave up.

Claire spoke through gritted teeth. "Perhaps there is some mechanical malfunction."

"Nothing wrong with this old truck but driver malfunction." Seth's voice was carefully calm, as though he'd waited to release the words until the anger had cooled.

Claire had been surprised and pleased that Seth himself had elected to teach her how to drive.

Now, she wasn't so pleased. He acted like driving was very easy, and truthfully, Claire had expected it to be. Didn't young teenagers do it? Maybe that was it. Driving should be learned while one was young.

One more time Claire cranked the motor and released the clutch, and one more time the engine coughed and died. A pungent gray-blue cloud dissipated in the late afternoon breezes.

Seth said nothing, but gazed out to the unplowed fields beyond the storage shed. In the silence, frightened crickets tentatively resumed their whining buzz.

"I'll bet the weeds that have grown around the truck are caught in something," Claire suggested. She could visualize them wrapped around some obscure but necessary truck part.

"Nope."

She wouldn't be beaten by some old piece of machinery. Jamming her feet on the pedals, Claire turned the key. To her complete surprise, she was able to shift into first gear. "It's moving!" She turned to Seth in triumph.

"Turn the wheel!" He leaned over to grab it and they lurched past a pecan tree, just missing the trunk.

The lower branches scratched against the windshield, startling her, and Claire released both pedals at the same time. The truck hiccuped to a stop.

Hand over her pounding heart, Claire exhaled. "I don't think I'm cut out for driving."

"Sure you are," Seth insisted, but there was a note of doubt behind the reassurance.

Claire looked back the way they'd come and saw the pale yellow grass that had been trying to grow under the truck. "We could have been killed."

"Not at that speed. Would have banged up the truck, though."

And put an end to any question of her driving. She should keep that in mind. Unfortunately, starting the truck proved to be a fluke. She couldn't even get the engine to turn over.

"Probably flooded the motor. We're not going anywhere for awhile." Seth reached across her and removed the key from the ignition, to Claire's annoyance.

What? Did he think she was going to try practicing on her own and hurt herself?

Probably.

"'Bout time for me to feed the ostriches." Seth offered her a strained smile and got out of the truck.

After a beat, Claire followed. "Thanks for taking the time to try to teach me to drive," she called, jogging until she caught up with his long-legged strides.

"No problem." He turned and touched the brim of his hat in obvious dismissal.

Claire's steps slowed and she watched as he crossed the gravel yard.

She was about to go out of her mind with loneliness. Long-distance calls to Audrey were both comforting and frustrating. While Audrey was always glad to hear from her, Claire got the distinct impression that she wasn't missed as much as she'd like to be. She also felt a jealous pang or two to hear Audrey sing the praises of Claire's replacement, who was also a struggling designer.

Claire waited to hear that some of her customers were clamoring for her latest designs. Audrey mentioned nothing, and Claire could just see the interior of the shop with some unknown's designs filling the displays and Claire's in the back on the fifty-percent-off rack.

Out of sight, out of mind.

They'll be sorry, she thought. Just wait until she got to Paris and became the latest rage.

So she wouldn't appear pathetic, Claire forced herself to cut back on her calls to Audrey, and there were some days when Seth was the only human being she spoke to.

After their argument, Seth had made it a point to stop by the house before he left Bellingham. He never wanted to linger, and though he was faultlessly polite, Claire knew he was eager to return to his own ranch. Was he still angry with her? Claire didn't think so. In fact, his gaze would linger on her as he said goodbye.

But he was sure keeping his distance

No one else had paid her any attention at all.

Well, she was working on that. She'd covered one overstuffed chair and had sewn miles and miles of piping for the sofa, which she was tackling next. As soon as the area rug she'd ordered arrived, Claire would have the wives over for coffee. They'd see she intended to keep her word about staying for the entire year, and that there was no reason they all couldn't get along. They could learn from each other, though Claire wasn't quite sure yet what knowledge she had that could be bartered for their company.

Leaning against the weathered porch railing, she fanned her face. While the nights were pleasant, the afternoons were hot. The barn must be stifling. Claire gazed from it to the house and came to a decision.

Her grandfather had laid in an apparently inexhaustible supply of root beer, and Claire decided to take a bottle to Seth in the ostrich barn.

She found him in Phineas and Phoebe's run. He didn't notice her at first, which allowed her to study him.

Tall, dark and handsome. She sighed. Talk about a fizzled romantic opportunity. Claire shook her head at her naïveté. She'd actually thought he might be interested in her. She'd actually thought that she, a city girl, could swoop into town, dazzle the prize catch for a year, then fling him back into the matrimonial pond.

The area ranchers were supremely unimpressed to have a budding New York designer in their midst. How could she dazzle anybody when she could go days without speaking to a human being in person?

Her city skills were useless out here. No one cared about whether hemlines were up or down or shoulders were padded or not.

Speaking of shoulders... Seth wielded a sack of ostrich feed and the muscles across his upper back rippled nicely. A girl could lean on a set of shoulders like those.

Claire's hand slipped on the wet root beer bottle and she remembered why she was standing at the fence. "Hi," she called softly, not sure whether she wanted him to hear her or not.

Seth heard her. Glancing up, he stopped scooping out feed and watched her for brief moments before resuming his task.

Claire felt awkward. She'd expected him to return her greeting at the very least. Should she leave? Stay outside the run? Join him in there with the ostriches? Phineas and Phoebe had spotted Seth and were on their way over, so Claire decided to remain outside the fence.

In a moment, he approached her, stripping off leather work gloves as he walked. "Is that for me?" He nodded to the root beer.

"Yes."

"Thanks." He took the bottle from her and drained it in one long draw. "Hot out here," he commented as he handed her the empty bottle and proceeded along the perimeter of the ostrich pen.

After that sparkling conversational exchange, Claire was ready to give up and return to the ranch house, but the thought of endless days spent alone with no one but talk show hosts for company propelled her to follow him.

"What are you doing?" she asked.

"Looking for Phoebe's latest egg while the birds are over there eating. She lays about every other day."

"Would they just leave their eggs like that? Shouldn't Phoebe be sitting on the nest or something?"

He favored her with a half-smile. "The male does his share of sitting on the eggs."

"Really! How modern of him."

"I knew you'd like that." Seth stopped and gingerly nudged at a mound of grass with his boot.

"Of course. In fact, I think men could learn a thing or two from ostriches."

"I think men can learn from ostriches, too."

An enlightened cowboy? How refreshing. "You agree?"

"Certainly."

Claire beamed until she saw the sparkle in his dark eyes and the suppressed grin at the corners of his mouth. "There's got to be a catch. What is it?"

A grin eased across his face. "Did I mention that out in the wild, the male builds his nest and then mates with as many females as he can and convinces them to lay their eggs in his nest?"

"We could deemphasize that part."

Seth abandoned the grass pile and continued scanning the ground. "The dominant female runs off the others and makes certain her eggs are in the center of the nest in the best position. The male can cover forty to sixty eggs, and any on the outer fringes act as a buffer to predators."

"A typical male fantasy, to have females fighting over him," Claire said in disgust, and Seth laughed.

He didn't laugh often, and the sound of it warmed Claire, even though he was amused at her expense.

They'd reached the end of the enclosure and turned the corner when Seth spied an area where grasses and dirt had been clumped together. Squatting, he carefully brushed aside bits of dried grass to reveal a shallow basin in the sand and a single ostrich egg.

"How many is that now?" Claire asked.

"Six." Picking up the egg, he walked to Claire and handed it to her over the fence. "Take this on into the shed for me, will you?"

"Sure." Claire set the empty root beer bottle down and reached for the egg.

"Here, let me take that." He traded her the egg for the bottle. "Wouldn't want it to get broken. These birds would try to eat it."

"Glass?" Claire cradled the egg as if it were gold. In a way, it was.

"Anything. In fact, while you take the egg, I'm going to check this pen for trash. You wouldn't believe what they'll swallow."

"Yes, I would. Phineas tried to eat my earring, remember?" *And remember that you held me in your arms?*

Seth looked at her, holding her gaze. "Yeah."

He did remember. Feeling her cheeks heat, she lowered her eyes to the egg in her hands.

"What do I do with this?" Claire wanted to get rid of the egg as soon as possible. What if she tripped and dropped the darned thing?

"Put it on the table with the scales. I'll be in soon."

Obediently, Claire made her way to the shed, terrified that she'd bungle this simple task.

The egg was a creamy color and heavy, with small dimples over its surface. Seth had brushed off most of the sandy dirt, but the egg by no means resembled the snowy white ones she purchased in the supermarket. Or had purchased before she'd made the arrangement with Mrs. Stevens. Now there was a thought. Claire had no idea of the ways of chicken laying, but shouldn't she be due some eggs soon? She should call Mrs. Stevens.

Claire stepped inside the shed and immediately sneezed. Horrified, she felt her hands involuntarily squeeze the egg and examined it closely for cracks. All was well, except for her nose, which itched. What a time for her allergies to kick in.

She concentrated on finding the table without mishap and set the egg on a folded towel before looking around.

There'd been some changes since she was last in the old barn. The walls had been removed from three horse stalls, and a webbed flooring had been installed. The wooden gates were replaced with wire fencing.

"For the chicks." Seth answered her unspoken question from behind her.

She hadn't heard him come in.

"We're thinking of trading some of our fertilized eggs for hatched chicks. We're getting a late start on the season."

"Why would somebody trade their chicks? Wouldn't that be helping the competition?"

"They'd end up with more eggs than we would chicks." Seth rolled up his shirt sleeves. "When the eggs hatch in about six weeks, they'll realize a seventy-five percent profit." He turned on the water at the stainless steel sink and proceeded to scrub his hands and arms all the way to the elbows.

Claire stepped back so water wouldn't splash on her turquoise silk blouse. Silk was not a good ranch fabric, but she was running out of clothes to wear. Her dry cleaning-bill was going to be huge. "Well, why don't you just wait until our eggs hatch?"

"I could and I may." He grinned as he dried his arms. "But I'm impatient." He walked over to the egg Claire had set by the scales.

She followed him, thinking how pleasant it was, just the two of them. Thinking that if she offered dinner, he might accept. Thinking that she had nothing appropriate to feed a man who had put in a hard day of physical labor.

"There haven't been as many men around the last few days," she commented, curious to hear his response.

"Roundup. Everybody's working cattle."

She'd forgotten all about roundup. Or hadn't ever known much to forget in the first place. "What about *your* cattle?"

He shot her a look before placing the egg on the scale. "I'm going to ride out to camp after I finish up here."

Claire blinked. His workday wasn't over. "Is...is the camp far away?"

Without looking at her, he shrugged a shoulder. "Sort of."

And he'd spent a chunk of the afternoon with her in the old truck. "Seth, you should have said something. You don't have time to teach me to drive now."

"Nobody else does, either, and you need to know how."

True. Claire tried not to feel guilty. How was she supposed to know it was roundup time?

As she tried to think of something to say, Seth turned on a slide projector. "What are you doing?" It seemed safest to stay on the subject at hand.

"Candling the egg. But because these shells are so thick, we need a strong light. A slide projector bulb works just fine." He held the egg in front of the light.

"What are you looking for?" she asked.

"To see if the egg has an air pocket...and it does." He smiled with satisfaction. "Look there."

Claire saw nothing but a dark blob, but the dark blob seemed to please Seth, so she nodded.

"That air pocket will get bigger and bigger as the chick gets nearer to hatching," he said, stooping to place the egg in the incubator. "The air supply lasts about thirty hours, which is how long they take to hatch."

"That long?"

"It's a tough shell."

After closing the door, Seth straightened. Their eyes met and they shared a smile, which Claire felt all the way to her toes.

She stood next to the metal incubator with the examining table at her back. Seth was directly in front of her, close enough for her to smell the soap he'd used and a faint whiff of root beer.

She couldn't move back and she couldn't move forward and Seth apparently wasn't going anywhere.

He drew his hands to his waist and studied her, his brown eyes revealing nothing of his thoughts.

Was he waiting for her to speak? Somebody ought to say something. Somebody ought to give somebody else a clue as to his thoughts. If somebody was interested in somebody, wouldn't he like to know that somebody else was interested back?

Or perhaps *some*body was overreacting and should get out of his way.

But instead of stepping to one side, Claire stayed where she was, waiting for Seth to make the next move. She secretly hoped that next move would be a kiss, but knew it wouldn't be.

And it wasn't. A second or two passed before Seth reached behind her and flipped off the slide projector light, leaving the fan humming in the silence.

His action brought him as close to her as he could get without touching her, and Claire had to force herself from moving that fraction of an inch that would bring them together.

She had to say something. She couldn't just continue to stand here and gawk at him, and she wasn't going to fling herself at him, either.

He raised his eyebrows a fraction and Claire realized she was being prompted. She cleared her throat. "Would you like to stay for dinner?" She hoped he'd accept and prayed that he wouldn't. Tuna fish and an apple was hardly what you fed a man you hoped to impress.

He blinked, then sighed. "I sure would like to, but I just can't this evening." Real regret sounded in his voice. "Gotta get to camp."

Claire let out the breath she hadn't realized she was holding. "Right. The roundup." She'd forgotten.

"That's right."

Neither of them moved. "I'll take a rain check, if I may?" Seth asked, and Claire responded with a huge smile.

"Sure. Anytime."

His eyes held hers for a moment longer and then he gestured to the side.

At that moment, Claire realized she was blocking him in, and had been since he'd put the egg into the incubator.

She turned quickly away. How humiliating. He probably thought she'd done it on purpose. Maybe she could pretend she hadn't noticed that she'd trapped him.

They passed the converted horse stalls and Claire blurted out a question to distract Seth. "You said you're getting some chicks? When?"

"After Phoebe lays a few more eggs," she heard him say. She didn't dare look at him.

"But this week or next," he continued as they exited the barn, "we're getting a couple of younger birds. Older yearlings."

"More ostriches?" She risked glancing at him.

He wasn't looking at her. "We're going to put them in that pen on the other side of the barn." He pointed.

"I didn't realize you were buying any more birds this season." She'd thought cash was tight.

"We hadn't planned to, originally, but we want to start getting a return on our investment as soon as possible."

He didn't say, but Claire realized it was because the ranchers would need money to buy the ranch from her at the end of the year. Again she felt guilty, though she shouldn't. It was their decision.

But shouldn't it have been her decision, too? She had as much invested in this venture as anyone else. More, even. She was all alone. If they didn't succeed, she'd inherit a bankrupt ranch, and then what would she do?

And where had the money to buy the new ostriches come from? One thing she'd learned about ostriches was that everything connected with the birds seemed to cost a fortune.

"These birds are eighteen and twenty-one months old and aren't proven yet, so they didn't cost as much," he explained, addressing her unspoken concerns. "In a few months, they'll start breeding, too. Then their value goes up."

"Well, I hope your gamble pays off," Claire said as they reached Seth's Jeep.

"I know you do." He touched the brim of his hat before climbing in the Jeep. "See you tomorrow afternoon. We'll make a driver of you yet."

"Oh—don't bother with that. I—"

"Claire." As he spoke, Seth sighed. "I've got to come out here anyway. An hour or two one way or the other won't make much difference to me."

Obviously the thought of seeing her didn't affect him in the slightest. Claire was hurt until she met his gaze. He was tired. She could see it in his eyes. And he still had work ahead of him. "In that case, may I have my key?"

"Don't hurt yourself," Seth cautioned as he reached into his shirt pocket and dropped the key into her palm.

"I won't." Taking two steps away from the Jeep, Claire raised her hand. "See you tomorrow."

Claire watched as the Jeep left the gravel yard and rolled onto the blacktop. By the time Seth arrived tomorrow, she was determined to be able to drive.

Taking a deep breath, which made her sneeze again, she turned on her heel and marched toward the red truck.

That evening, Claire fought the truck until she ran out of gas. Early the next morning, she got up, intending to waylay whoever arrived to take care of the ostrich chores and ask him where she could get gasoline.

She recognized the man who drove up, but didn't know his name. "Hi!" she called from the porch, when he slammed the door of his truck and started for the barn.

The man stopped and looked at her. Though his expression wasn't hostile, it wasn't friendly, either. If she'd met this man in the subway, she would have put serious distance between them.

But this wasn't the subway. This was Texas, where the people were friendly and open, she reminded herself, and gingerly climbed down the steps. Everyone had told her so. This man was just busy. Everybody was busy this time of year.

Claire approached him, a smile on her face. "Could you tell me where I can get gasoline around here?"

For a moment, she thought he wouldn't answer. He looked like he didn't want to. "Your tank empty already?" he asked at last.

"Yes."

The man shifted his weight and squinted off to the side of the ranch house. "What did old Beau use all that gas for?" he wondered aloud. "Truck came by our place about the same time and we're still half full."

"You have gasoline delivered out here, but we have to haul our own trash?" Claire asked in amazement.

The ranch hand stared at her a moment, then pointed. "You talkin' about *that* tank?"

Claire turned to see where he was pointing. A round tank sat on a platform. Hanging from the tank was a hose with a familiar-looking nozzle.

"No, I'm talking about the gas tank in the truck."

"Fill 'er up from there," the man said and headed toward the ostrich barn.

The old tank was so much a part of the landscape that Claire never really noticed it or wondered what it contained. The tank sat behind the garage with the tractor and other machinery, and since she wasn't about to operate any of that, she hadn't gone back there.

Now she did. Yes, it was a gas tank. No, that didn't help, since there weren't any operating instructions posted.

Claire sighed. She absolutely would *not* ask that ranch hand for help.

If it was the last thing she did, she was going to figure out how to pump gas into one of the orange gas cans lined up next to the garage, put gasoline into the old truck and then drive the truck over to the tank.

With luck, she wouldn't drive into the tank and blow herself up.

She could do this. She was strong. She was determined.

She was a Bellingham.

Picking up one of the five-gallon orange cans, Claire nudged the others in case one might be full. No luck.

After staring at the pump assembly, Claire carefully set the can down and went inside the ranch house. It was an excellent time to check with Mrs. Stevens about those eggs and, not incidentally, avoid making a spectacle of herself in front of the ranch hand.

Seth had given Claire a list of the area ranches' telephone numbers. She found the Stevens place and punched the number.

"Hello?" Mrs. Stevens answered, breathing as though she'd had to run for the phone.

"This is Claire Bellingham."

"Yes?"

She sounded impatient, and again Claire reminded herself that this was a busy time. "I was calling about eggs. We agreed that I could have some from the chickens I gave you?"

"Yes, Claire. Come and gather them whenever you like."

"Okay, but Seth will probably be the one to come get them."

"Seth? Good heavens, can't you tell that the poor man is run ragged as it is?"

"I wasn't going to ask him to make a special trip." Claire refrained from telling her that she had no way of getting to the Stevens ranch. That wasn't *their* problem. "So...how many?" How many eggs was she entitled to?

"How many do you need?" came the rapid question.

The woman *was* impatient. Claire couldn't ignore the edge in her voice. "A dozen will be fine."

"Sure. Anything else?"

Yes. Claire had hoped for a little friendliness, maybe even an invitation for a cup of coffee and a chat. But roundup or no roundup, it was obvious that Mrs. Stevens had no time for her. "No, nothing else," Claire said quietly and carefully cradled the telephone.

Pensively, she wandered over to the front window and stared out. She wasn't really looking at anything until her attention was caught by the ranch hand's departure. She half-expected him to check to see if she'd pumped her gas, but he didn't even look in the direction of the tank.

Within moments she was alone.

As she had numerous times, Claire tried to tell herself that everyone was busy and preoccupied, but it didn't make her feel any better.

These people acted like they resented her, and she couldn't figure out why. If anything, she would have thought they'd be eager to see that she was happy and comfortable.

Didn't she hold their future financial security in her hands?

She was going to have to discuss the ranchers' resentment with Seth, and soon.

But first, she was going to learn how to drive.

CHAPTER SEVEN

FIGURING out how the pump worked and then actually getting the truck started and running gave Claire an intense feeling of satisfaction. Only the first time someone bought one of her designs had she felt this accomplished.

She drove in circles around the yard, honking at Phineas and Phoebe as she passed. The birds scuttled to the far end of their run, and Claire guiltily drove onto the blacktop.

There, she practiced going forward and backward. Wouldn't Seth be surprised when he arrived for their lesson?

Stunned, probably.

Just as that thought occurred, Seth's Jeep Cherokee turned from the main road onto the blacktop.

She was driving on a road with an oncoming vehicle. Not quite ready for traffic yet, Claire pulled over to the side of the road—way over. So far over that her tires sank into the soft shoulder. She stopped and waited until Seth pulled alongside.

"Hey, look at you!" he said, a wide grin splitting his face.

"Yeah, look at me, stuck in the dirt," Claire said, ruefully.

"But you got the old girl going. That's something."

He looked so pleased with her that Claire couldn't help but respond to his praise. She grinned at him and felt a warm glow spread through her middle.

Propping his elbow on the open window, face framed by a cowboy hat, Seth was one good-looking man.

Once again, Claire marveled that the rugged outdoor type appealed to her. Who'd have thought it? The problem appeared to be that the sophisticated, big-city type didn't appeal to him.

Seth pulled his elbow in. "Turn her around and come on back to the yard. It's time you learned advanced maneuvering." He drove off, obviously assuming Claire was capable of turning around.

She hadn't practiced turning around. She'd practiced honking and driving in wide circles and moving forward and backward. No turning large vehicles on narrow roads.

First she had to get onto the road.

Cautiously, she pressed the accelerator, turned the wheel and felt a jolt as the truck bounced onto the road. In the rearview mirror, she saw Seth park and get out of his vehicle. Leaning against it, he crossed his arms over his chest and waited.

He made her nervous. She didn't want him watching her attempt her first tight turn, so Claire did what she knew best, which was forward and reverse. She backed down the drive until she passed the turn, then drove forward into the yard.

"Showing off, eh?" Still grinning, he got into the truck.

He thought she was showing him her progress instead of avoiding turns. After he left, she vowed, she would practice turns.

Seth made her practice coming to a full and complete stop, signaling and weaving around various obstacles. Then he moved the tractor out of the garage and made Claire drive in and out.

After only about half an hour, he pronounced himself satisfied with her progress for the day.

It was what Claire had hoped for. "Since we're quitting early, do you have time for a quick bite of supper?" Good grief. She was beginning to sound country.

Seth glanced from her to his watch and back to her again, obviously considering whether to accept or not.

Claire had tried to make the invitation sound casual and offhand because the tuna casserole she'd fixed didn't deserve anything more. She wanted Seth to stay because he wanted to, because he might enjoy being with her, not because he thought he *had* to. "The casserole's already cooked and is just staying warm in the oven," she coaxed, since he seemed hesitant. "Table's all set and I just have to heat up the green beans." And this time she was certain they were green beans and not pickled okra.

"Sounds good." He gave her a half-smile and nodded. "I'll feed the birds and be right in."

He was going to stay! Claire raced into the kitchen. She'd been plotting and planning all day. After he ate, when they were lingering over coffee and the sugar cookies she'd baked—another milestone—she'd mention the attitude of the ranchers toward her and see what Seth had to say.

Her own dishes had arrived, and she was proud of the table, though the black and white geometric pattern looked odd in the homey country kitchen. In a way, though, it represented her. City stuck in country.

She turned her attention to the food. Tuna noodle casserole, canned green beans and canned peaches. Claire sighed faintly, then cheered. As soon as she got her driver's license, she could replenish her groceries and fix him something really terrific next time.

Besides, she'd managed to salvage at least a dozen whole, unburned cookies from the batches she'd baked today.

She was just about to peek out the front window when Seth's shadow grew across the wall.

"Something smells good," he said, as he pushed open the screen door. "I'll be with you as soon as I wash up." He gave an approving nod to the table as he walked past.

Fighting flutters of nervousness, Claire had everything ready by the time he returned.

"I hardly recognized the room back there." Seth hooked a thumb over his shoulder. "You do all that yourself?"

"Yes." Claire offered him the serving spoon. "As soon as I finish the sofa and the curtains, and the rug arrives, I plan to have a coffee for the ranch wives. I've only met Mrs. Stevens." She tried not to make it sound accusatory.

Seth helped himself to a huge portion of her casserole. He was obviously an optimist. "That's real nice of you."

She watched anxiously as he took a bite, then relaxed when he smiled at her.

"It's good."

Silly to feel so happy with his comment. What else could he say, really? But when he ate his entire portion and unself-consciously helped himself to more, she felt proud.

Pumping gas and baking all in one day. How far away her former life seemed.

"So how's roundup going?" she asked.

Seth shrugged. "It's going."

Claire didn't know whether that meant it was going good or going bad.

"And how's your work going?"

It wasn't going. Claire hadn't drawn or sewn a single piece of clothing since she'd arrived.

In fact, no ideas at all had struck her. Usually, something would trigger an idea and a garment would pop full-blown into her head. She'd grab the first available piece of paper and draw furiously, then go back and refine later. Living at the ranch obviously wasn't conducive to new ideas, but she wasn't ready to panic yet. If she finished redecorating without one new idea, then she'd panic.

"I haven't quite settled down to work yet," she answered. "I'd just finished assembling a portfolio for the Paris contest I told you about. If I'm a finalist, I have to submit a new body of work according to the assignments the committee gives me."

"More drawings?"

"Yes, and finished samples, as well." Somehow, the prospect didn't fire her imagination the way she might have expected it to. Right now, she was content to sit here, in an authentic country kitchen, and watch Seth devour food she'd prepared for him.

These domestic twinges weren't nearly as bad as she'd always thought they'd be.

As he ate, Claire told him a little about her work and how important it was to develop a signature style. "I can't seem to settle on any one thing," she concluded. "I hope that by studying the craft and being around other designers, I'll figure out which direction I want to go."

Seth scraped his plate clean and declined her offer of more food. "When should you hear if you're a finalist or not?"

"July."

"You've got awhile to wait, then."

Claire grimaced. "Yes, but I should be getting a head start with some preliminary drawings. There's only a month between the time contestants are notified and when their entries must be returned. That's not enough time to do it all from scratch."

"Well, I wish you luck." Seth drew the black and white napkin from his lap.

"Thanks." Claire refrained from adding that she'd need it. She planned to make her own luck.

"I suppose I ought to be getting on over to camp," Seth said, but didn't look as though he wanted to leave the table.

In the fading light, Claire noticed the shadows under his eyes and the deepening lines on either side of his mouth.

The man was exhausted. Flat-out exhausted.

"How about some coffee and cookies before you go?" she offered.

"I shouldn't, but I will." Seth smiled. "Make that coffee strong."

"Is there any other way to make it?"

That prompted a laugh as he pushed his chair away from the table and stood. "I've got a couple of phone calls to make. Mind if I use your phone?"

"Go ahead." Claire got up from the table. "If you like, I'll bring the coffee to you in the other room."

Dinner had gone great, Claire thought as she busied herself grinding beans and brewing coffee. This, she *did* do well.

Pulling cups out of the cabinet, she wrestled with how to bring up the subject of her ostracism by the ranchers. Or if she was imagining the whole thing. She didn't *think* so. Maybe it was because when she first agreed to stay, she was so afraid they'd expect her to run Bellingham that she made too much of a point about her work. Maybe they thought *she* was busy and were worrying about bothering her.

And she would be busy, *should* be busy, but there had to be a middle ground.

To give Seth privacy on the telephone, Claire started washing the dishes, waiting until the coffee was brewed before going into the living room.

She arranged a tray with cups and saucers, cookies and sugar—she was out of milk, except for some ancient powdered stuff—and carried it into the living room.

"Ready for coffee?" she asked brightly. Good grief, she sounded like a flight attendant.

Walking around the ugly sofa, Claire set the tray on the battered coffee table. "I hope you don't use cream in your coffee, I'm all out."

Seth didn't respond.

She looked at him.

He lay sprawled across the sofa, his head on a corner pillow, one leg carefully propped on the cushions so his boot wasn't touching the fabric.

And he was fast asleep.

Claire was so surprised that she stayed in the stooped position over the coffee tray for several seconds waiting for Seth to rouse.

When he didn't, Claire straightened, noting the slow rise and fall of his chest and the deep resonance of his breathing.

What should she do? "Seth?" She called his name softly, thinking that if he'd merely dozed off, the sound of his name would startle him awake.

But Seth apparently hadn't just dozed off. Here lay a man so bone-weary, he'd passed out as soon as he'd stopped moving. Fortunately, he'd fallen asleep on Claire's sofa instead of in his truck as he drove to the campsite.

He needed sleep; he'd get sleep. Silently, Claire sat in the stuffed chair she'd recovered and watched him.

The handsome rancher must be carrying a heavy load. He obviously worked a grueling schedule and seemed to be involved in even the smallest details of ranching and the ostrich project.

Which was odd, now that she thought about it. Why was the head of the ranchers' coalition doing routine ostrich chores? Shouldn't a hired hand be assigned that task?

Seth had flown to New York. Seth had scheduled the lawyers' visit. Seth had looked after getting Beau's house cleaned. Seth had even had her boots repaired.

A horrible thought struck her. Seth must be doing everything himself because there wasn't anyone else available to do it.

As she watched him sleep, Claire puzzled over the situation.

She knew that funds were tight. Wouldn't it be logical to assume that the area ranchers couldn't afford to hire many hands? In that case, Seth ought to be hiring help, not buying those yearling ostriches.

And, too, Claire had become Seth's responsibility. She, who was worthless in this environment. Seth had promised her that he would take care of everything. Claire wouldn't have to deal with the ostriches at all.

She thought back to that day in the ostrich barn. Seth probably would have promised her anything to ensure her cooperation.

And he was exhausting himself trying to keep his promise.

Why had it taken her so long to realize what the other ranchers and their wives must have seen?

No wonder they resented her. Justified or not, they blamed her for Seth's exhaustion.

It's not my fault!

Plop them down in the middle of New York City and see how *they'd* fare.

And if they were so all-fired angry about Seth's heavy workload, then why didn't any of them come out and help? Because Seth hadn't asked them to, she surmised, watching him sleep. He probably figured they had enough on their plates as it was.

During the few minutes she'd watched him, he hadn't even twitched, and she couldn't bear to wake him just yet.

Pouring herself a cup of coffee, she sat back in the chair and studied him.

In sleep, his rugged face was relaxed and the lines that furrowed his brow had eased. People depended on him and looked to him as a leader, but was anyone looking after Seth, the man?

Claire remembered what it had felt like being held in his strong arms against the muscled chest and sighed, admitting to herself that she'd like to be held in those arms again. And not because he was comforting her, either.

What sort of woman would attract a man like Seth? Reviewing all she knew about him didn't yield much. Claire sipped her coffee and grimaced. She preferred it with milk, which reminded her that she had no idea how Seth took his coffee.

Or his women.

If the local girls had appealed to him, wouldn't he have married one of them by now? Claire had only to look at the long, lean form on the sofa across from her to know that he'd had ample opportunity to be fruitful and multiply.

Well, whatever kind of woman attracted him, Claire bet it wasn't one who planned to run off to France the first chance she got.

She took another sip of coffee, then grabbed for a cookie to get the taste out of her mouth.

She ought to wake him up. If he slept too much longer, he'd be out for the night. Setting her coffee on the table, Claire brushed the cookie crumbs off her hands, reached down and gently nudged Seth's shoulder. His body absorbed the contact without response. His breathing didn't even change.

"Seth?" she whispered and knelt next to him.

He drew a long breath, releasing it on a sigh. His head settled deeper into the sofa pillow.

"Poor guy," Claire murmured. "You're everybody's white knight, aren't you?" Impulsively, she smoothed the dark hair off his forehead, then allowed her fingers to trace his cheekbones and jaw, stubbled with the day's growth of beard.

A corner of his mouth twitched upward, drawing her attention.

Claire, don't, warned an inner voice even before she'd thought about kissing him.

Once the thought occurred to her, Claire couldn't get it out of her mind. *I might not get another chance*. She *had* to know what his lips would feel like against hers.

But what if he woke up while she was kissing him? How could she possibly explain? She'd embarrass them both.

Unless he kissed her back.

The possibility that he might encouraged her to lean forward. At the last moment, Claire detoured and placed a chaste kiss on Seth's forehead.

He didn't stir.

Claire lifted her lips a fraction of an inch before moving to his temple, then his cheek. Seth's breathing remained slow and steady.

Hers, however, sped up. To ease the strain on her thigh muscles, Claire carefully propped her arm on the other side of his chest and shifted her weight.

The movement of the cushions didn't wake him, so she lowered her lips to his jaw and the corner of his mouth. Then she waited, holding her breath.

Not even Seth's eyelashes flickered, so Claire settled her lips against his.

She meant to kiss him quickly and pull away, her curiosity satisfied, but once she touched her mouth to his, she knew a quick kiss wouldn't be enough.

Then she heard it—a tiny sound deep in his throat. Claire froze, afraid her luck had run out.

But in the next moment, she found that her luck had just begun.

Seth's lips moved beneath hers, and Claire savored the feel of them before reluctantly pulling away.

A split second later, he murmured unintelligibly before sliding his hand up her arm and pulling her back down.

Claire gasped as her elbow bent and she collided with his mouth. It was a rough landing, but Seth adjusted quickly and teased her lips apart.

Was he awake? Still asleep?

Did she care?

Not at the moment.

Claire closed her eyes and simply enjoyed the heavy weight of Seth's arms across her back and the feel of his mouth moving against hers.

If this was a sample of his unconscious kisses, she shivered to imagine how he kissed when he was fully awake.

She nestled closer, only to feel him pull away.

He mumbled something that sounded like, "Night, darlin," before struggling to turn onto his side.

Claire used the moment to scoot out from under his arm, and Seth finished turning, his calves still hanging off the edge of the sofa.

Whew. Rocking onto her heels, Claire waited for her heart to slow. They were definitely going to have to try that again when he was awake. In the meantime . . . *Sweet dreams, cowboy*.

Silently, she stood on shaky legs. Seth was obviously out for the count. Claire gathered the coffee things and carried them into the kitchen. He might be angry in the morning, but she was going to let him sleep tonight, or until he awoke on his own.

Should she check on the ostriches? Seth had probably planned to look in on them before he drove away. Grabbing the flashlight that hung by the back door, Claire decided to see that all was well, not that she'd necessarily be able to tell if all *wasn't* well, but at least she could reassure Seth that she'd checked.

It was dusk, with a lighter sky than she'd expected. Still, she could see the first stars. It was Claire's habit to step outside before going to bed. The black sky with the swirls of white stars fascinated her. The lights of the city and the tall buildings kept her from seeing the stars. She'd almost forgotten that they were there.

Tonight's evening sky was a gorgeous canvas, with pinks at the horizon deepening into purples, navy and finally black.

And suddenly, Claire didn't see a night sky in Texas but an evening gown—literally a gown of the evening. She caught her breath, wanting to drop the flashlight and race into the ranch house for paper. Instead, she raised her face skyward and absorbed the sight, knowing she wouldn't forget her first original idea since coming to Texas. Claire let out a sigh of relief. She'd been afraid she wouldn't have any more ideas.

The pinks had disappeared before she finished her walk to the barn. Everything looked fine to her, and Phineas and Phoebe seemed content, though she wasn't certain what an uncontent ostrich looked like.

Back at the ranch house, she paused by the front window and saw that Seth was in exactly the same position in which she'd left him. He'd be better for the sleep, she told herself, and entered the house by the kitchen door.

As soon as she finished the dishes, she was going to draw that dress and hope the Fashion Academy asked its finalists for evening gowns. But then it didn't matter whether they did or not. This was a dress Claire wanted to make no matter what.

She was scouring the casserole dish, lost in thought about possible fabrics, when a loud ringing startled her and she dropped the dish into the water.

The wall telephone. She hadn't heard the telephone ring since she'd moved here. Who could be calling her now?

"Hello?" she gasped, out of breath. She hadn't even bothered to dry her hands.

"Claire?"

"Yes?"

"This is Pete Stevens. Is Seth around?"

Naturally, the call wouldn't be for her. "Yes, but he fell asleep. Let me see if he's awake yet."

She peered into the living room, using the window reflection to see that Seth hadn't roused. "Listen, Pete, I've already tried to wake him once." Twice, actually, but she wasn't going to mention that. "He's exhausted."

"Best let him sleep, then. The man's been working too hard. We were just wondering where he was."

"Conked out on my sofa." Claire thought it best to mention Seth's exact whereabouts so there wouldn't be any misunderstandings.

"Well, pull off his boots and throw a blanket over him and he'll be fine."

Claire laughed, then rashly blurted out, "Since he's here, don't bother sending anyone over to do the chores tomorrow morning. We'll take care of it."

"All righty." Pete's voice was full of approval, the warmest she'd ever heard it.

Hanging up the telephone, Claire wondered what would happen if Seth awoke during the night and left. Well, if that happened, then she'd just have to feed the ostriches herself. She had no idea what else was to be done to or for the birds, but at least she could keep them from starving.

After finishing the dishes, Claire found a quilt for Seth in the chest at the foot of her grandfather's bed. The smell of cedar clung to the fabric, and it was soft from many washings.

Had her grandmother sewn this quilt? she wondered, admiring the thousands of tiny stitches forming rings and petals as she carried it into the living room. What a seamstress, she marveled, studying the design.

She shook out the quilt, preparing to lay it over Seth, then stopped at the sight of his boots. Pete had said to take them off, but she'd prefer to leave them on rather than risk waking him. On the other hand, he'd be more comfortable with them off.

Draping the quilt over the back of the sofa, Claire took hold of one brown boot heel and pulled. And pulled more. And twisted and tugged and yanked. When the boot finally slid off, Seth's leg dropped to the couch with a thump. Claire held her breath, certain he'd wake up. At first he appeared to because he drew his other foot upward and took that boot off himself, to Claire's relief, but then he fell back against the pillows.

Exhaling, Claire gently arranged the quilt around him, smiling when his nose wrinkled at the cedar scent.

"Good night, cowboy," she whispered and went off to draw her gown.

Though Claire was enveloped in a creative fog until the wee hours, she set her alarm, thinking Seth would awaken early. She wanted to catch him before he left.

After the alarm went off the next morning—or later that same morning—she batted at it and listened.

Silence. Seth must be gone then. Maybe he left her a note.

Claire stretched, slipped her feet into backless slippers and went to investigate.

In the early morning light, she saw the lump of the quilt and felt slightly disappointed that Seth hadn't folded it before he left. She would have sworn he'd be the type to do so.

After she got closer to the sofa, she realized he hadn't folded the quilt because he was still underneath it. Asleep.

Claire blinked. He'd slept nearly ten hours and she still didn't have the heart to wake him.

She wanted him to wake to the smells of breakfast, though she didn't know what she could fix without milk or eggs. Well, if not breakfast, then coffee and . . . and she'd do the ostrich chores. All by herself.

She'd show him she wasn't completely helpless and she'd send him back to his ranching buddies all rested.

Moving quietly out of the living room, Claire dressed and crept to the barn.

Ostrich food came in big sacks like dog food. Though Claire didn't know how much to feed ostriches, she dragged the sack to the fence and scooped out what she intended to be a generous amount. Phineas and Phoebe had spotted her. Claire had no intention of getting in the pen with the birds. She couldn't reach Seth's regular feeding spot, so she flung the feed in as far as she could and hoped for the best. Next she checked their water supply and added some. Any eggs Phoebe had laid, she could keep today, Claire decided.

The incubator appeared to be incubating, so Claire returned to the ranch house, feeling very accomplished.

Now for her next challenge, breakfast. After consulting her cookbook, Claire decided to attempt biscuits because they didn't require eggs. How ironic. One ostrich egg would solve her problems. She could make omelets for an army.

She was tempted, really tempted, but Seth would probably strangle her.

And she'd fix bacon. Seth had originally brought her bacon, and Claire hadn't used any of it. Now she would. Humming softly to herself, she got to work.

The smell of frying bacon—okay, smoking bacon—finally woke Seth. Claire couldn't have asked for a better situation. There she was, looking domestic with her hands coated in flour as she rolled out her second batch of biscuits, when a rumpled Seth appeared at the kitchen door.

"Good morning?" He didn't sound all that sure.

"Good morning!" Claire trilled too brightly. "Want some coffee?"

"Uh, yes." With a sheepish smile, he reached out to take the mug she handed him. His eyes slid to the side at the same moment a scorched smell reached Claire.

Turning, she whisked the frying pan off the heat. She hoped he liked his bacon crisp and his biscuits hard. And his milk powdered.

"Claire?" He ran his hand through his hair.

"Yes?"

He stood in the doorway, looking appealingly uncertain. "Is there anything I should apologize for—other than falling asleep in the middle of dinner?"

"No." She should apologize for taking advantage of him while he was asleep, though, but she wouldn't. "I could tell you were tired, so I let you sleep. I hope you aren't angry."

"No." He sipped his coffee and winced. "Pete."

"He called. Everything's fine."

Seth muttered and shook his head. "Then I guess I'll clean up and feed the birds."

"I've already fed the ostriches." Claire had been looking forward to making the announcement.

His eyes widened. "*You* fed the ostriches?"

She nodded, pleased with herself.

"This morning? All by yourself?"

"You needed the sleep."

"Well, thanks." He stared at her, his expression indicating that he was seeing her in a different light. "You're all right."

Meaning he hadn't thought she was all right before. But it was a compliment and she'd take it. Afraid she'd blush, Claire turned to her biscuits. "Better hurry, or your breakfast will get cold."

All in all, it wasn't a bad breakfast. Claire had found some homemade blackberry preserves in the pantry. The sweet jelly softened her biscuits so they could actually be eaten, and Seth ate more strips of bacon than she could count. He didn't seem bothered that the bacon was in little bitty crunchy pieces, either.

Afterward, they checked on Phineas and Phoebe, and Seth complimented her.

Claire, basking in the warm glow of approval, was feeling altruistic. "Look," she began, as they walked to his Jeep. "Checking on the ostriches wasn't really all that hard or time-consuming. Why don't I take on the evening feeding from now on? The exercise will do me good.''

Seth stopped. ''Are you sure, Claire?'' He studied her closely. ''It may look easy now, but when those chicks hatch, there'll be a lot more work.''

''That won't be for a while, will it?''

He shook his head.

''We can talk about it then, okay?'' She wanted to see him as rested-looking as he was now. Ostrich care wasn't on her agenda, but she could devote a couple of hours a day to the cause.

They reached his Jeep. ''Okay, then. I'll let you give it a shot. And I'll stop by when the new birds get here.'' He smiled, his gaze sweeping over her. ''Thanks, Claire,'' he said as he climbed in the Jeep.

She felt all warm and mushy inside. Seth had smiled at her and spoken more to her this morning than he had the entire time she'd been at Bellingham.

Just before he drove off, he snapped his fingers as though he'd forgotten something. He got out of the truck, strode purposefully toward her and stopped.

''What?'' Claire asked.

''This.'' Cupping her face with his hands, Seth brought his mouth to hers in a hard, searing kiss.

Claire was so stunned, she forgot to kiss him back.

Seth released her just as suddenly, and she had to grab onto his forearms to keep from falling.

A slow smile spread across his face. ''We *have* progressed to this point, haven't we?'' he asked, his voice slow and liquid.

He *knew*. She didn't know exactly how much he knew, but he sure knew something.

Releasing her, he touched the brim of his hat and winked. Then he strode across the gravel yard, got into the truck and drove off, leaving Claire wondering what would happen between them next.

CHAPTER EIGHT

FEEDING the ostriches wasn't so bad, Claire decided after several days of the chores, except that she hadn't seen Seth.

Perhaps it hadn't been in her best interests, as far as seeing him was concerned, to have volunteered for ostrich duty. She hardly knew what she'd say when she did see him, though. How could she explain kissing him when she thought he was asleep?

And how could he explain pretending to be asleep?

Claire grinned. Guess that made them even.

He *was* thinking of her, she knew. The ranch hand who'd arrived to do the chores the next morning delivered a sack of groceries containing milk, among other much-needed supplies. He also handed her a booklet with Texas driving regulations so she could study for her driver's license exam.

For the next few days, Claire practiced driving, studied, finished covering the couch and started sewing the curtains. At night, when the stars were out, she drew versions of her evening dress, none of which satisfied her.

Everything she'd designed in the past several years had been attention-getting, because Claire wanted attention. The quickest way for a designer to build a clientele was to have a celebrity appear in public wearing one of that designer's creations. Celebrities wanted to be noticed, therefore Claire had designed clothes that would get their wearer noticed in a crowd.

But there weren't any crowds out here on the ranch. The life-style was slower. More basic, with a different sort of energy. Strong, not frenetic.

She studied the drawings spread out on the kitchen table. As usual, she'd tried to design a distinctive dress that would catch the eye. She rather liked the black one with the giant stuffed silver lamé star. The purple one with ribbons hanging from the bodice and silver stars at the ends was an attention-getter, too.

They all shouted, "Look at me!" There wasn't a quiet dress in the lot.

No, wait. There was one, but the sketch with tiny stars spread on a navy background looked too much like polka dots on a spring church dress instead of an evening gown. Too subtle, too precious. Too yuck.

Claire sighed. Nothing here captured the feeling of twilight or capitalized on the gorgeous colors of the sunset.

Picking up the first drawing, the one with the giant star at the shoulder, she reduced the size of the star. Less dramatic, but more wearable. One didn't have to shout to be noticed, she realized for the first time. Hmm. And she decided to ditch the black. Everybody did black, but the sky wasn't all black. There were billions of stars.

Claire imagined a dress with the Milky Way swirling over it and shook her head. She didn't want a dress for a science fiction convention.

This dress would take more thought, but for now, it was bedtime. Morning came early when hungry birds depended on you.

Her new rug and the yearling ostriches arrived at the same time on the same day.

A horse trailer pulled into the yard, followed by Seth's Cherokee and a brown delivery van. Claire and Seth could only exchange a wave before each became occupied with the deliveries.

Claire pulled furniture aside to make room for the long, heavy roll of carpet. The driver stood it on end next to the hat rack. Claire signed the receipt, hoping he'd offer to help her move furniture and unroll the carpet, but he didn't.

And she still had to roll up the old rug, too. Glancing out the window as the van drove off, Claire saw that the ranch hands and Seth were totally involved with the new birds—gawky teenaged ostriches. The men probably hadn't even noticed that her rug had arrived.

Claire carried all the smaller furniture into the kitchen, then pushed the couch to one side and tipped it over as she'd done when she'd covered it. The rug's color was more vibrant underneath the furniture, testifying that her grandfather hadn't rearranged the grouping in years, if ever. She'd also discovered different colors when she'd removed the old fabric on the furniture. From the seams, she'd learned that the ugly olive had been a kelly green and the tan had been a paler green.

Next to the bright patch of rug that had been under the sofa was a darker, dirtier place, and a chewed fringed edge where Blackie, her grandfather's dog, had lain. Down the center of the room, the nap had worn as people had walked from the front door into the kitchen.

Claire grasped the edges of the rug, then hesitated. It was silly to be sentimental over a dirty old carpet, but she was. The rug had a story to tell. For all she knew, it was the only rug that had ever been in the Bellingham ranch house. Maybe her grandmother had picked it out as a new bride. Maybe her father had crawled over it. Maybe those were his teeth marks in the corner of the battered wooden coffee table.

There was a worn spot next to where the easy chair had been. Claire knew from her previous visit that her grandfather spent his evenings reading or watching television while sitting in the chair. But he was gone now, and so was her father. Even Blackie was gone.

There was only Claire, some cousins and an aunt she'd never met.

Lifting the edges of the rug, she sneezed as years of dust billowed out. Ugh. Nothing to be sentimental about there.

After Claire cleaned the ancient dirt up, she wrestled with her new rug, cutting the twine and ripping off the brown paper that covered the roll. Crumpling wads of paper, she turned to throw it into a corner, then jumped at the dark shape outlined at the door.

"You startled me!" she exclaimed, when she recognized Seth and pushed open the door.

"I knocked, but you must not have heard," he said, an easy smile on his face as he stepped inside. He took off his hat and hung it on the rack by the front door. "Looks like you could use some help."

"I'd like to pretend that I'm big and strong and independent and send you back to your ostriches, but, yes," she admitted, tucking a lock of hair behind her ear, "I need help with this rug."

"That's what I'm here for," he said.

"Is it?"

Something flickered in his brown eyes, but it was quickly damped. "That and to introduce you to the new ostriches."

Claire snapped her fingers. "I knew there was a catch."

He frowned. "If you'd rather—"

"Seth." She grasped his forearm. "It was a joke. Of course I want to see the new birds." The instant she finished speaking, she became aware of the rock hard muscles beneath her fingers. Good grief. Slowly, she released him, surprised that even that brief contact had the power to affect her.

"Well." She shoved her hands into the back pockets of her jeans. "Let's unroll this rug and see if the colors work."

"You mean they might not?" Seth looked so unnerved that Claire laughed.

"I was working with swatches of fabric in New York and everything looked fine in the warehouse there, but you never know until everything is put together."

"Let's get it unrolled, then." As he bent down, Seth spoke. "I thought after I show you the ostriches, I'd drive you into town to take your driver's test. You've been studying, haven't you?"

"Yes!" She dropped her end of the rug. "But...but don't I need more driving practice? What about parking? And I've never actually driven on a road with other cars."

Chuckling, Seth waited for her to pick up her end of the rug again. "After you pass the written part, you'll get a learner's permit, unless you want to try your luck at the behind-the-wheel part today, as well."

Claire moved farther into the room. "Right here, I think." They set the rug down and nudged it open with their feet. "What happens if I don't pass the driving part of the test?"

Seth shrugged. "After a while, you can take it again."

Trying the test now sounded like it might be worth the gamble. "Do you mind if we practice a little before we leave?"

"Fine with me." He seemed in an easygoing mood today. More open. More approachable. Was it because of their shared kiss?

"Can you spare the time?" Claire asked. She didn't want a repeat of the evening when he fell asleep on the couch.

Or maybe she did.

"Thanks to you taking on those evening chores, my roundup is mostly finished, so I'm not quite as busy as I was."

"Oh, good. Does that mean the rest of the ranchers aren't so busy, either?"

"More or less. Why?"

"Now that the rug is here, I wanted to have the ranch wives over for a coffee." She lifted the edge of the easy chair so the rug would lay flat underneath. "Since I've been here, I've only met Pete's wife."

"That's nice of you." Seth glanced at her approvingly.

Claire felt such approval wasn't totally warranted. "I'm not just being nice, I'm forcing the issue. I don't know whether they've been afraid to approach me or they just didn't want anything to do with Beau Bellingham's granddaughter." She invoked her grandfather's name deliberately. For all she knew, they still resented the fact that she hadn't arrived in time for his funeral. "But they haven't been overly friendly, so I figured I'll make the first move."

Seth shot her a look, which Claire met calmly. He was her sole contact with the ranching community, and she wanted him to know that she was making an effort to fit in for the time she was here.

"Couldn't hurt," he commented at last, not conceding anything.

They finished unrolling the rug and Claire, hands on hips, studied it. Vaguely Oriental in design, a large, two-toned pink cabbage rose was in the center of a pale pink field banded with black and cream. It perfectly complemented the predominately black and pink floral she'd chosen for her upholstery and curtain material. What a relief. This, she could live with for the rest of her time here.

"Mighty fancy for this old ranch house." Seth rubbed the back of his neck in the time-honored tradition of a male confronted with something he didn't quite understand.

"Please. I just don't happen to like calico."

"Big investment."

By that, Claire deduced that he was concerned about the cost. "As a designer, I can purchase fabrics wholesale, which I did. And I sewed everything myself. The rug, yes, that was expensive, but when I sell this place, I want it looking appealing."

Seth stared hard at her. "I told you we'd buy the ranch from you." His voice was sharp with concern.

"So? Won't somebody be living here? How about the people who'll be tending the ostriches?"

"Yeah, you're right."

He visibly relaxed, and Claire gave him points for not mentioning that rural ranch families probably wouldn't share her exotic tastes in decorating. She also reminded herself how important the success of this venture was to him. "Let's get the furniture into place."

"I passed! I can't believe I passed!" Claire gave a little hop on the sidewalk outside the Royerville courthouse.

Seth shook his head. "I can't believe you passed, either." Claire swatted at his shoulder. "I told you I'd been practicing."

He grinned. "Congratulations."

"Thank *you* for teaching me."

"No problem." He gazed at her. "Want to celebrate with lunch?"

He was finally asking her for a date. Well, not exactly a date, but after weeks of being more or less ignored, Claire would count it as one. She slipped her arm around his. "Thank you kindly, sir."

Seth took two steps, then stopped, looking from the old red truck to Claire's feet. "Hank's place is just around the corner. Want to walk?"

"I can't believe this!" she exclaimed in mock indignation. "The state of Texas says I can drive, but you really don't trust my driving, do you?"

He gave her a sheepish grin. "It's the parking I don't trust."

Claire wasn't fond of that part, either. "Okay, let's walk."

Seth still wore his cowboy garb of that morning. But for her first trip off Bellingham since she'd arrived, Claire had put on one of her short skirts, silk blouses and flats, since the heels she would have preferred to wear might have interfered with driving. She also added big loopy earrings and her red lipstick. Her hair was a mess because it desperately needed a trim. However she didn't think that was the reason people were staring at her.

Maybe it was because she was with Seth, but he'd smile and nod to acquaintances, who nodded back, then openly stared at Claire as though she were some unknown species.

"Why are people staring at me?" she asked him as they slid into booths at Hank's Barbecue. "Is my skirt too short or something?"

Seth's eyes twinkled. "*I* think your skirt is just fine."

Which meant it was too short. Not in New York, perhaps, but definitely in Royerville, Texas. Obviously her reputation had preceded her, and from the looks she'd received, that reputation was tarnished. Coffee invitations would definitely go out this week.

Claire picked up the laminated menu and sighed faintly. Endless variations of meat and sausage, all accompanied by beans and potato salad. She ordered a barbecued sandwich.

Seth placed his order and sat back, studying her. "You know, I'm thinking that getting your license and the new ostriches calls for a bigger celebration than this. Are you free for dinner this evening?"

Claire nearly choked. He was asking her out. For real. At the last minute, true, but he wanted to spend time with her. "Well, I have to feed Phineas and Phoebe." She couldn't *believe* she'd said that.

But Seth appeared to think her concern was appropriate. "I'll send someone to take care of them."

He smiled. "I know a restaurant you'd like, but it's quite a drive."

Now *this* was a real date. "Do *I* get to drive?" she asked playfully.

Shaking his head, Seth took a swallow of iced tea. "No, but I'll let you drive us home after lunch. By the way, this restaurant is fairly dressy. You get to put on the dog."

"I beg your pardon?"

"Bring out your fancy duds, ma'am."

"Would these be Western duds?" Claire visualized square dancing. She couldn't even fake one of the full-skirted costumes. Maybe she could work with jeans and boots . . .

"No, I believe one of your New York ensembles would be more appropriate," Seth told her, dropping his Texas drawl.

"Be still, my heart." Life was just getting better and better.

"Figured you'd like that."

Who would have thought such a jewel of a restaurant would be out in the middle of nowhere?

The Wainright Inn boasted a French chef and an extensive wine list. Claire was dressed in her favorite black dinner dress and squired by a tall, dark and handsome man. All was right with the world.

"I'm not much of a wine drinker," Seth told her candidly, when they were settled at a tiny table on the terrace overlooking a waterfall. "And something tells me you might know a bit more about wines than I do."

"I've taken a couple of courses," Claire confirmed.

He passed the book over to her. "Then have at it."

She looked at him in surprise. "Really? You want me to order?" Most men would be too insecure to admit to a lack of knowledge about anything. But Seth didn't have any reason to be insecure, did he?

"Sure. I'll even skip my usual bourbon and branch."

She grinned, then hefted the book. "Oh, my." The wine list was the size of a telephone directory.

"If you like, consult with Mr. Wainright and see what bottles he's got open this evening. That way, you can sample several kinds by the glass. We'll order food to go with the wine."

Claire was in heaven. How many times did she get an opportunity like this?

With Mr. Wainright's enthusiastic and knowledgeable help, Claire spent fifteen wondrous minutes choosing wines and food. Several times, she glanced at Seth, who was spreading an alarming amount of pâté on toast points. "Go ahead." He gestured. "I'm enjoying myself listening to you two."

After they ordered, Claire sat back. "Thank you."

He inclined his head. "You're very welcome."

"No, I mean it, Seth. This is..." She searched for the right words.

"Like home?"

She laughed. "I didn't eat like this all the time."

"But I imagine it's more what you're used to," he observed quietly.

The waiter brought crab-stuffed mushroom caps and the sommelier arrived with a white wine, giving Claire time to think of a response. She didn't want him to think she was pining away on Bellingham, but she wasn't embracing the life of a rancher, either.

She met Seth's eyes. "Moving here was a big adjustment for me, and I'll admit that I miss some aspects of my life in the city. But there are certain compensations."

And one of those compensations was sitting across the table from her. Wearing a crisp white shirt and a dark suit, Seth looked just her type. When he spoke, his deep voice wrapped her in its warming rumbles, and his eyes pulled her into their smoldering depths. He found her a desirable woman and was letting her know it.

Pretty heady stuff.

As course after course arrived, Claire chattered about her life and her dreams, breaking all the popular magazines' rules about encouraging the man to talk about himself.

But she didn't care. She felt wonderful, the best she'd felt in weeks. Perhaps the wine had something to do with it, perhaps not. She didn't care.

She never wanted the evening to end, but of course, it had to. The sommelier arrived with two tiny glasses of a dessert wine with an orangy bouquet.

"Oh." Claire closed her eyes and leaned her head back. "This is the *best* one. My favorite."

A corner of Seth's mouth quirked upward. He was drinking coffee. "You like that one, do you?"

"Mm." Potent and sweet, it was the kind of wine she could easily drink too much of. "Would you like some?"

He shook his head. "I'm driving."

"A taste, then." Claire held the dainty glass to his lips.

His eyes on hers, Seth sipped the tiniest amount. "Now that packs a kick."

And so did he.

Claire swallowed. What was she doing, flirting and carrying on with Seth? Hoping it would lead somewhere, that's what.

But where? In a few months, she was going to Paris, and she didn't want to leave her heart behind. Excusing herself, Claire made a beeline to the powder room and gave herself a stern talking-to.

Seth wasn't the kind of man to trifle with a woman. A lesser man would have thought a woman in Claire's position would be ripe for a no-strings affair, but Seth wasn't a lesser man. He didn't have no-strings trifling in mind.

Claire couldn't have misinterpreted the look in his eyes tonight or her response to it. She felt attractive and desirable for the first time in a long time.

She could fall for Seth, she thought suddenly, and stared at herself in the vanity mirror. Fall for him as in white picket fences and two-point-two children.

And live the rest of her life on a ranch.

No. She was overreacting. She was going to Paris. *Remember Paris,* she instructed herself.

And any attraction she felt for the handsome rancher should be attributed to her isolation and the fact that he was good-looking and eligible—the only eligible man for miles around. That was it. She wasn't falling for anybody.

Claire snapped open her black beaded bag and withdrew her lipstick. Painting her mouth a vivid red, she looked more like the old, sophisticated Claire. Adding more eye shadow helped, too. And she was going to have to back off on the giggles and the little touches. Cool things off. Let Seth know she enjoyed his company, but as a friend, nothing more.

Yeah, right, but she'd give it a try.

When she returned to the table, Seth stood. "Ready to go?"

When she nodded, he put his hand in the small of her back, which was left bare by the deep V of the dress.

Claire had to restrain herself from purring against him.

Mr. Wainright himself saw them out, handing Claire a package.

"Three bottles of the dessert wine you liked so much," Seth said in answer to her raised brow.

"Seth!" Delighted, she threw her arms around his neck, forgetting all her good intentions.

She kissed his cheek, leaving a red imprint, then tried to wipe it away with her fingers.

Catching her hand, Seth kissed the palm before releasing it.

Uh-oh.

They stared at each other, blocking the doorway, until a smiling Mr. Wainright cleared his throat and opened the door for them.

The rush of warm night air broke the spell, and they both blinked, then laughed self-consciously.

Claire had carried on a monologue during dinner, so on the hour drive to her ranch, she was determined to draw out Seth.

"How come there isn't a Mrs. Seth Montgomery?" she asked with great tact.

He didn't seem to mind the question. "There almost was once."

"What happened?"

He waited so long to answer that Claire suspected she'd gone too far. "We were both too young. I went off to college—"

"And studied . . . ?" Claire interrupted.

"Ranch management."

Naturally. She should have guessed.

"I was three years older than she was, and we got engaged when she was still in high school. I had another year of school, and rather than sit around and twiddle her thumbs, she decided to go away to school for a year while she was waiting."

"And met somebody else."

"Eventually, but mostly she discovered that there was a great big world out there and she wanted to see some of it. We postponed the wedding so she could go to school another year, and *that's* when she met somebody."

"I'm sorry."

"Nah. It's for the best."

And he was pining away for her. That's why he'd never married. Warning bells sounded. Obviously, Seth was a man who didn't love lightly. Claire had suspected as much. Now she knew.

"What's her name?" For some reason, Claire was slightly jealous of this woman Seth had loved, and she didn't want to keep thinking of her as "that woman."

"It was Trisha Stevens. She married a guy named Abernathy. Lives in San Francisco."

Trisha Stevens. *Stevens*. "Pete's daughter?"

Seth nodded.

It must have been an amicable parting, since he was still close to Pete and his wife, and the older couple thought so highly of him.

"So how come you haven't married?"

"I want to, eventually, but not until I get to Paris. It's just taking longer than I thought."

They were silent after that, each lost in thought. As they drove down the highway, only the headlights from oncoming traffic illuminated the rolling landscape. More stars than Claire had seen in her life twinkled down, reminding her of the evening dress. And when she thought of that, she thought of Paris. In less than a year, whether or not she won the chance to study, the sale of Bellingham would finance her trip. Claire's long-held dream might actually come true.

And then what? Just getting to Paris didn't guarantee success, and Claire hadn't ever considered what would happen after she arrived. Just *getting* there had seemed like a big enough goal.

Now, thanks to her grandfather and the man sitting next to her, it was time to think about another goal.

Claire must have dozed, because her head jerked upright when Seth's Cherokee jounced off the paved road into the gravel yard. How embarrassing. "Great companion I am," she mumbled, hoping that her lipstick hadn't smeared and there weren't wrinkles in her cheek.

"You had a big day."

"And you've got a twenty-mile drive home. How about some coffee?"

She expected him to refuse, but he pulled up next to the house and turned off the engine. When he got out of the car, Claire quickly inspected her appearance in the rearview mirror. Not too bad. Not great, but not too bad.

Neither spoke as they climbed the rickety porch steps. After unlocking her front door—she couldn't break the lifetime habit of locking her doors—Claire flipped on the light and swept her gaze over the living room. She'd replaced the lamps and the worn wooden pieces with her own black lacquer lamp tables and stone pottery lamps.

Seth gave a low whistle. "Look what you've done with this place." He looked at her. "You've got a real knack for colors and fabrics."

"I'd better, considering my chosen profession." She patted the sofa, indicating that he should sit while she made coffee.

This time, when she brought in the tray, Seth was wide awake.

They chatted easily. He didn't stay long, but it was the perfect ending to a perfect evening.

She followed him to the door. During the last few minutes, she'd watched his gaze follow her lips as she talked. If he kissed her, it would seal the change in their relationship that had begun this evening.

Claire's heart started pounding as Seth reached the door and turned to face her.

They stared at each other, much as they'd gazed into each other's eyes at the doorway to the restaurant.

"I'm thinking that I'd like to kiss you good-night," Seth murmured, his deep voice barely audible.

"And I'm hoping you will," Claire whispered in response, abandoning all the resolutions she'd made in the Wainright Inn powder room.

Seth bent his head, and Claire tilted hers back—way back, since he was so tall and she'd kicked off her shoes earlier.

The instant his lips met hers, her knees weakened and Claire wrapped her arms around his neck so she wouldn't lose her balance. This had the happy effect of signaling her surrender to Seth.

He deepened the kiss, teasing her lips apart with an ease that spoke more of finely honed instincts rather than a technique learned with much experience.

She'd take instincts over mechanics any time, was Claire's last rational thought.

Asleep, Seth wasn't a bad kisser, but awake . . . She nearly melted when his hands caressed her bare back, and stood on her tiptoes, trying to get closer.

"Claire," he breathed, holding her against him.

She was doomed. She knew it. She shouldn't be kissing him this way, as if she were parched and he was rain. In the weeks ahead, somebody was going to get hurt.

It might even be her.

CHAPTER NINE

"Coco, you clever girl. Is that an egg I see?" Claire stood at the edge of the immatures' pen. Recently the male ostrich's beak had turned bright red, as did the skin on his shins, signaling that he was ready to mate. Whether or not he actually would was up to Coco.

Both Coco and Christian—Claire had named them for Coco Chanel and Christian Dior—had come from early breeding stock, and Seth had hoped they might begin laying sometime this year. That's why the ranchers had gambled and bought the birds.

In the month since Coco and Christian had arrived at Bellingham, Claire had never been in the pens. She'd never been in with Phoebe and Phineas, either. The ostrich's two-toed foot with its evil-looking claw intimidated her. Seth had warned her how hard they could kick, and she didn't want to find out firsthand.

But there was that lovely egg. Wouldn't Seth be surprised and pleased?

He was coming over today at noontime, and Claire was looking forward to seeing him. They were officially on ostrich-hatching watch. The first three eggs had been removed from the incubator and placed in the hatcher, and any day now, Bellingham would have its first ostrich chick.

According to Seth, that would be when the real work started. They would have hatching eggs, new chicks and new eggs, each with different chores.

She sighed. She hardly saw him for any length of time now, as it was. There had been no more fancy dates, although they'd eaten a few quick meals together. The longest time she'd spent with him had been the Sunday he'd come to help her clear overgrown weeds and grass around the garage and toolshed. They'd planned to spend the whole afternoon together, but there had been phone calls for Seth, then a couple of the ranchers had visited the ostriches and stayed to help clear the weeds.

It hadn't been quite the romantic day she'd planned, though it spoke much of the different attitude of the ranching community toward her.

As she waited for Seth, Claire thought back over the month that had passed since their evening at the Wainright Inn.

She'd given her coffee for the wives, and at first thought no one would come. Claire had issued her invitations by telephone in an attempt to strike up conversations with the women. Though each expressed a polite pleasure in being asked to Bellingham, none of the women accepted on the spot. Most gave her deliberately vague responses and promised to get back with her.

Seth had asked about her coffee, so she told him the date of the Saturday morning she'd planned to have it. But when he asked if she expected a crowd, she was only able to shrug. Within hours, his mother called to tell her that she would be delighted to attend. By the next afternoon, nearly everyone else had managed to clear their schedule, as well.

Claire knew Seth and his mother must have had something to do with all the women finding that particular Saturday morning free, after all, but she pretended to her guests that she didn't.

Amazingly enough, the very subject Claire thought would set her apart from the ranch wives—her designing—was what brought them together. The women sewed quilts for charity auctions and were impressed with Claire's needlework. With their encouragement, she brought out some of her designs and sketches and was promptly invited to join their quilting group. This time, instead of turning down the invitation, Claire just as promptly accepted, thrilled with the opportunity to learn quilting from experienced quilters.

She'd been meeting with them twice a week ever since.

They adored her fabric scrap bag, which she gladly shared, fascinated as they discussed various patterns. In fact, the leftovers from her decorating project were to be used in an appliqué quilt. The roses would be cut out, arranged in a new pattern and pieced into the fabric of a quilt with the same color scheme. Far from being intimidated by the bold design, these women applauded it. Claire was sheepishly forced to abandon her preconceived ideas about ranch women.

And out of her quilting experiences came ideas for satin and velvet quilted evening jackets.

And then denim skirts and jackets using the satin and velvet scraps.

From there, it was a natural progression to leather, which Claire had discussed with the quilters last night.

Now she eyed the ostriches in front of her. Ostrich leather had a distinctive bumpy look. Although Bellingham was years away from producing enough birds to support a steady leather supply, it wasn't too early to create a demand for it. In fact, Claire could be in the forefront of a new industry. The idea appealed to her. A lot.

In the meantime, though, Coco and Christian had presented her with an egg and Seth hadn't arrived yet.

There wasn't any reason Claire couldn't collect and process the egg herself. She'd watched Seth do it lots of times. Neither Coco nor Christian was paying the slightest bit of attention to her or their egg. If Claire got it, then it would save Seth time—time they might spend drinking some of her grandfather's unending supply of root beer and talking.

Before she could lose her nerve, Claire unlatched the gate and slipped inside. Walking slowly and keeping near the perimeter, she moved toward the live oak tree that grew between the two ostrich runs. Phineas liked that spot for his nest and must have told Christian about it.

Keeping her eyes on the ostriches, Claire concentrated on moving slowly, but she still managed to catch their attention. Too late, she realized they must think she was going to feed them.

Both the older pair and the younger first-time parents approached.

Claire forced herself to breathe calmly. Seth and the men went in the pens all the time. She'd just take the egg and walk out like she knew what she was doing.

"Howdy, guys." She tried to talk Texan to them. "Hey, there, Coco. Congratulations. I didn't even know you were expecting. You should have said something. Phoebe and I would have thrown you a shower."

They were looking at her, blinking their beady eyes with the long eyelashes.

Claire didn't want the egg anymore. She wanted out. There was no way she could climb the flimsy wire fence.

"Tell you what. I'll just leave you two alone to celebrate and let Seth steal your egg. Maybe since this is your first one and everything, Seth will let you hatch it yourself."

Though she spoke to Coco, it was Phoebe who spit at her.

"Hey! What did you do that for?" Totally repulsed, Claire grimaced and backed away. "I'm not even in your pen. And have *I* ever taken one of your eggs? Have I?"

Two of the birds hissed, she wasn't certain which two.

Great. "It's okay." She held up her hands. "I'm leaving."

She turned around and walked, increasing her speed as she heard ostrich footsteps behind her.

And then she felt it—one of them nipped her on her rear end!

She screamed and whirled.

Startled, Coco backed off, but Christian nipped at her jeans again.

This time, Claire swallowed her scream and batted at the big bird. "What are you doing? And in front of your wife, too. You ought to be ashamed of yourself."

He went for her again. Yelping, Claire started to run. She was ostrich bait. They were tired of that dry pellet junk and were trying to supplement their diet with a hunk of nice, juicy Claire.

"Claire!" She heard Seth shout and saw him wave to her.

"He's after me!" she wailed, stumbling.

Seth ran into the ostrich pen. "Are you hurt?"

She flung herself at him and felt his heart pound against her ear. Christian pecked her again. "*Ow!*"

"It's your jeans." Seth turned her so he could shield her from the ostrich. "Go on out."

"But—"

"Go."

Though she didn't want to wimp out and abandon him, Claire took off.

Within moments, Seth joined her as she panted against the wooden fence post. "What's going on?" he asked. "What were you doing in with the ostriches?"

"Coco laid an egg and I was trying to get it."

Seth's face lit up. "She did? This is great. Her mother was an early layer and still produces over ninety eggs a season."

Claire tried not to be miffed that he was spouting ostrich stats instead of consoling her.

"I was concerned that old Christian might not be up to the job, if you will."

Rubbing her backside, Claire grimaced.

"Oh, hey." He tried to see behind her. "Are you all right?"

It was a little late in the day to be asking, but Claire forgave him. "I'll live. Why was he pecking at me?"

"He was going after the brads in your jeans. Remember, they'll eat anything shiny. Look at mine." He gestured down at himself, and sure enough, his jeans didn't have any of the small rivets at the stress points.

"He did the same thing to you?"

Seth nodded. "The older birds did. That's why I'm careful what I wear when I'm around them."

"I thought I was doing great to remember to take off my jewelry."

"Don't forget buttons, too."

"Okay." She looked at her blouse. "I suppose I should be grateful he didn't peck at these." The buttons on her blouse were handmade of painted clay. She'd sewn the shirts and an artist had made the buttons in a brief collaboration one season.

"Yeah." Seth reached out as if to touch one of the buttons, then must have thought better of it. Shoving his hands into his back pockets, he cleared his throat. "Well, I'm off to get that egg. Where was it?"

"By the tree."

Shaking his head as he opened the gate Seth said, "That tree's going to give us trouble when it starts dropping acorns. We'll have to keep the area swept so the birds won't eat too many of them."

Claire nodded, thinking of the unending list of potential pitfalls connected with raising ostriches.

Back in the converted barn, Seth carefully put the new egg in the incubator, stood back and sighed. "I think this ostrich business is really going to work, Claire."

"You've always said it would work."

He grinned. "Yeah, but now I'm starting to believe it."

She planted her fists at her waist in mock indignation. "You mean you've been *lying* to everybody?"

"Not lying, but I have my down days just like anybody else."

Claire couldn't imagine Seth Montgomery, savior of the Royerville ranchers, having doubts.

He moved over to the hatcher. "There are so many diseases they can get. You know, if you dip the eggs in a solution that's too cool, the insides will contract and pull any surface bacteria through the pores to the inside of the egg." He rubbed his forehead. The gesture was one she'd noticed him make when he was fighting fatigue. "Once the chicks hatch, we'll have a whole new set of problems. And we need to find buyers." He sighed. "Sometimes it's tough to keep going."

"And yet you always do."

He smiled at her. "That's mostly because of you."

A warmth spread through her.

"I keep reminding myself that you moved all the way here because I convinced you I could make this work. You believe in me."

Well, yes, but she didn't deserve all that credit. "Remember that my grandfather didn't leave me much choice."

"You had a choice," Seth insisted. "You could have chosen not to come, but you didn't." His knuckles brushed her cheek, and Claire could smell the disinfectant on his fingers.

In the next instant, Claire forgot about the barn and ostrich smells as she realized that Seth was going to kiss her and that she wanted very much to be kissed.

"You're my strength, Claire," he whispered just before his lips met hers.

The magic was still in his kiss, but Claire also felt uneasy. She was his strength? She'd thought she was a burden. Lacking any ranch skills, except her newly learned quilting and her rudimentary cooking, she wasn't cut out for ranch life.

Claire squeezed her eyes tighter and stood on tiptoe, trying to deepen the kiss and bury all the distracting thoughts.

Seth moved his arms around her and hauled her to him before kissing the side of her neck and her temple, and then just holding her. "Sometimes I don't know how I managed everything before you came into my life."

Claire stiffened involuntarily. His feelings for her were much deeper than she'd imagined. Seth wasn't a demonstrative man, but she should have seen this coming. She'd known all along that Seth wouldn't spend the energy on dead-end flirtations. And while he wasn't actively seeking love, when he found it, he expected a life partner. Someone to support *his* goals and dreams.

She couldn't stay at Bellingham and be his support and strength. She had other plans for her life, plans that would take her away from him.

Seth loosened his hold. "What is it?"

"I—" How could she warn him not to fall in love with her?

Just then, she heard a quiet rustle and grabbed onto him, peering around to see if it was a rat or a bug or something.

He chuckled. "You're just not an animal person." Fondness sounded in his voice.

"No, I'm not and I never will—that egg moved!" She pointed to the hatcher. "It moved all by itself!"

With his arms still around her, Seth turned to look. "Hey!" He grinned at her and gave her a final squeeze. "Looks like our first chick wants to come out and see the world."

* * *

Claire had no idea that ostrich hatching was so fraught with peril. Or that it took so long. Or that it required monitoring. Constant monitoring.

After fixing dinner, serving it and cleaning up, Claire joined Seth in the ostrich barn.

"Remember me telling you the air sac in the egg would last about thirty hours?" Seth asked. "Well, the bird has got to break through that hard shell and get his beak to air or he'll suffocate. If he takes too long, we have to help out."

Claire could understand that, but wasn't this a natural process? "What happens to them out in the wild? People don't wander around with needle-nose pliers helping ostrich chicks hatch."

Seth shrugged. "The chicks don't all make it, and ninety percent are killed by predators anyway."

"Oh. Well, then after the ostrich beak is out, will everything be okay?"

"Mind you, I haven't been through this myself, but I understand that the membrane inside can get thick and sticky just like glue. We'll have to wash the birds off, but you don't want to drown them, either." He stared at the quivering egg, then pointed to another one. "There's another egg ready to hatch."

Eyes bright, Seth turned to her with a huge smile. He was so obviously excited by the whole process that Claire couldn't help but smile at him.

"Why don't we just cut the egg open?" she asked.

"Might hurt the bird. You can tear the vessels that attach it just like in a human baby, and it'll bleed to death."

"Never mind."

In the end, as soon as the tiniest hole in the egg appeared, Seth used his pliers and enlarged it. "I can't believe they can get out at all. This shell is like iron."

Claire brewed coffee. It was almost midnight, but she could tell they weren't nearly done yet.

"That other egg doesn't seem as active as this one was," she commented as she handed Seth his mug.

"I noticed that, too." He frowned. "Hope it's not breech."

"You mean there's a right way to come out of the egg?"

"Sure." His look was solemn. "If the egg sac and the beak aren't on the same end, the chick has nothing to breathe."

Setting his mug down, he stood by the hatcher and stared. "I don't like it." The second egg was nearly motionless.

Carefully taking a hammer and using the pliers as a chisel, Seth tapped at the egg. Nothing happened. He tapped harder, then gave it good whack.

Claire gasped. What if he'd stabbed the chick?

"Keep an eye on the other egg for me, will you?"

She could see the baby ostrich's entire head. "Looks like the chick is resting. He's probably exhausted."

"Can't rest too long," Seth said as he tried to pry a hole in the second egg, "the membrane will harden."

At last, he managed a jagged hole in the shell and picked up the egg to examine it under the lights.

Swearing, he set the egg down and immediately went to work on the other end. "Bird's upside down."

"Does that happen often?"

A drop of sweat trickled down the side of Seth's face. He used his shoulder to wipe it away. "No. We just ran into some bad luck."

Seth wasn't as careful opening this end of the shell.

"Is the chick still alive?" Claire asked when she saw the beak.

"Don't know yet. I think so." Seth continued to chip away at the shell. "Claire?"

"Yes?"

"If you could find another pair of pliers, why don't you work on the first egg? I'll feel more comfortable when the chick is out of the shell."

"Me?" He trusted her, the original ostrich klutz?

"If you don't mind?" He gave her a weary smile, and Claire took off to find her grandfather's tools.

By the time she'd returned, bringing the coffeepot with her, Seth had exposed half the bird. It was alive, but weak.

Her chick hadn't progressed.

"I don't know if that's a bad sign or not," Seth said before filling his mug and draining half of it. "Since I don't have any experience with hatching, I guess we'll just have to play it by ear. Why don't you get to work on the shell?"

For the next hour, they worked in silence, except for the chipping sounds they made breaking pieces of the shell.

Claire's wrists and hands ached long before her damp chick emerged and lay exhausted in the warmer.

"He's so big," she said, feeling like a midwife.

"By the time he's three months old, he'll weigh a hundred pounds." Seth carried his chick and placed it in the warmer, as well.

"Your chick doesn't look so good." Claire stated the obvious.

"We need to clean them off and then I'll chip them."

"Isn't that what we just did?"

"No." Seth smiled faintly. "I've got a gizmo here—" he turned to the shelf and picked up a metal device that looked like an ear-piercing gun "—that will implant a microchip in their necks that identifies them by sex, genetic makeup and when they hatched."

"You're kidding. Can you use it to control them, too? Like little ostrich robots?"

"Claire." He chuckled and put the microchip gun on the shelf. "It just helps us keep them straight. Once the birds are grown, there isn't really any way to tell how old they are. Also, we want to avoid inbreeding."

"So, are we decorating in blue or pink?" she asked, already thinking of names.

"Vet'll have to tell us." He reached for her and wrapped his arms around her waist. "Thanks, Claire." He dropped a kiss on the top of her head. "You've been great."

Claire nestled against him, thinking that, yes, she *had* been great, and that she'd enjoyed the hours spent working with Seth. Helping him these past weeks had given her a satisfaction she'd never known. She felt needed. No one had ever needed Claire before, and she liked the unfamiliar feeling.

The sun was just peeking over the horizon when Seth and Claire finally left the ostrich barn. The chicks were in the warmer, and it looked as though they'd both survive the experience.

"I'm going to fix us the biggest breakfast you've ever eaten," Claire announced.

"I'm ready." Seth sounded as tired as she felt. "Maybe you could skip the eggs, though."

She chuckled as they climbed the porch steps. "You got it."

Claire noticed something stuck inside the screen door about the same time Seth did.

"What's this?" He pulled out a thick but mangled envelope and handed it to her.

At the sight of the return address, Claire's hands went cold. "It's from the academy." Her heart picked up speed. All her other letters from the academy had been thin.

"Looks like it's had quite a trip."

"From France." The letter had originally been sent to her address in New York, then forwarded. "Why wasn't it in my mailbox?" she asked, scared to open it in front of him.

"Mabel, the postmistress, must have thought it looked important and ran it out on her way to work this morning."

"That was nice of her." She looked at him. They still stood on her front porch, and Claire knew that she was going to have to open the letter. If it was good news, she could share it with Seth. If it was bad news, he'd make her feel better.

It was already partly torn. Claire stuck her finger in the hole and pulled, destroying the envelope.

With trembling hands, she unfolded the packet and found the letter.

We are pleased to inform you... was as far as she read before bursting into tears.

CHAPTER TEN

"CLAIRE, what's wrong?" Seth drew her shaking body close.

"I'm a finalist!" Frantically, she wiped at her eyes so she could read the rest of her letter. Somewhere in the back of her mind, she noticed that Seth had said nothing.

After congratulating her, the academy's judges instructed her to submit four samples of her work, with sketches. One design for day, evening, resort wear and one of her choice.

"I can do this!" She looked at Seth, who had been reading over her shoulder. "In fact, I should have been able to predict the sort of designs they'd ask for." Flinging her arms around him, she squeezed. "I'm going to Paris!" She wanted to shout. To sing. To dance for joy. Here was her chance. All she had to do was reach out and grab it.

"Congratulations." It was the most insincere word Claire had ever heard him utter.

She dropped her arms. "Aren't you happy for me?"

A flash of some dark emotion flickered in his eyes. "Of course I am." He dipped his head and kissed her on the cheek. His lips were cold. "This is what you've always wanted."

"Yes." Claire stepped back. "It is." What was the matter with him? No matter what he said, she knew he wasn't as thrilled about her finalist status as she was.

"When would you go to Paris?"

Ah, that was it. He was worried that she'd leave the ranch before her year was up. "I haven't been selected yet, but if—*when* I am, the exact date would be up to the designer who'd sponsor me, but I wouldn't leave before next spring."

She expected him to act relieved, but he only gave her a tight nod and turned away. "Listen, I think I'll skip breakfast and just head on back to my place."

"Are you sure?" Claire touched his arm, and he looked at her. "I can cook fast. I've been practicing."

Now his smile was genuine, but he still shook his head. "I'm bushed, but I'll check in later today."

Lifting his hand in farewell, Seth strode down the stairs and to his Cherokee. He drove off without glancing back at her.

Well, what was bothering him? Claire wondered as she walked into the ranch house. She was at a loss to understand Seth's cool behavior.

She'd been happy for him as each ostrich milestone was reached. She'd even helped with chores. And hadn't she just spent the night helping him hatch baby ostriches?

Now something good had happened in her career. Why wasn't he happy for her?

Collapsing onto the couch, Claire closed her eyes as the room spun. Exhaustion, that was it. They hadn't slept all night. Seth was exhausted. When he'd had time to rest, he'd act differently.

Finding an explanation that made sense let Claire relax. In a few minutes she'd get up and eat something, then plan what to submit to the academy. She sighed. Just a few minutes...

* * *

Shadows were lengthening when Claire awoke. For a second she couldn't figure out where she was, then she remembered and groaned. A whole day wasted. How much time did she have to get her designs to Paris, anyway?

She groaned again when she sat up and discovered her stiff neck. Rubbing it, she bent over and found the packet on the floor by the sofa. Unfolding the papers, she retrieved the letter.

"August twentieth!" That was less than a month away. The letter had taken two weeks to reach her. Two precious weeks.

"I can do it," she said aloud. She'd get started right now. Her stomach rumbled. Or she'd start after she ate something.

Seeing the dirty coffee mugs in the sink reminded her of the missed breakfast with Seth and his lack of enthusiasm at her news.

She wished she knew what was troubling him, but she couldn't worry about it now. She had to turn her attention to her designs.

Claire worked long into the night, and it wasn't until she was ready to sleep again that she remembered the ostriches. How could she have forgotten them?

Had they been fed this evening? What should she do? What about the chicks? She had no idea what to feed them.

Thus, Claire found herself in the ostrich barn in the wee hours for the second night in a row.

Someone else had been there, because the two chicks had been moved to a special pen and two more eggs were in the warmer, joining one that had already spent several days there.

Claire assumed that the older birds had been fed and hoped that Seth hadn't been the one to feed them. It would hurt her to think he would come to Bellingham and not let her know he was there.

By late the next day, Claire still hadn't seen him and wondered whether or not someone would come and feed the birds. Besides, she had no idea what she was supposed to feed the chicks.

Claire headed for the barn, then stopped. If he wouldn't come to her, there was no reason she couldn't go to him.

Before she could lose her nerve, Claire returned to the house. The weather was stifling, so she wore a silk shorts set she'd designed during her retro phase. Flared tap pants were topped by a midriff-baring tied halter top printed with red cherries and green stems on a white background. It wasn't a feed-the-ostriches outfit anyway, she thought as she put on lipstick, grabbed her purse and keys and headed for the old truck.

In spite of what she'd told Seth the day she'd passed her test, Claire wasn't all that confident of her driving skills. However, she encountered no one on the road from Bellingham to the Montgomery Rose.

Once she passed under the iron arch, Claire started feeling nervous. Her initial resentment had worn off and she suspected she was behaving childishly. So he hadn't raved about her news. She hadn't won anything yet, had she?

Look at this place. It was huge. Seth had far too much on his mind to care about Claire making the finals in a contest he'd never heard of.

But it still hurt.

She passed the ranch house and drove into the small office parking lot. Seth's Jeep Cherokee wasn't in sight, but she decided to go inside anyway.

The secretary was talking with a tall, gray-haired woman Claire recognized as Seth's mother. Both broke off and turned to Claire, who hesitated in the doorway. Impossible though it was, she had the oddest feeling that they'd been talking about her.

"Claire, how nice to see you again." Mrs. Montgomery stepped forward and held out her hand.

Claire had met the imposing matriarch of the Montgomery Rose when she'd attended Claire's coffee. Shaking the woman's hand, Claire wished she'd rethought her tap pants outfit. She was afraid she looked like a woman on the prowl.

"Did you come to see Seth?" Mrs. Montgomery asked. "I'm afraid he's not here."

Claire sighed. "I need to speak to him about the ostriches."

"Is there something wrong?"

Claire met the brown eyes of Seth's mother. *Yes*, she wanted to say, *only I don't know what it is*. "We need to discuss the feeding schedule. Is someone coming this evening?" *Is Seth coming this evening*?

The older woman gazed at her a moment, then smiled. "Viv," she said to the receptionist, "I'm taking Claire over to the house. We'll be there if anyone comes looking for us."

She didn't say Seth's name, but Claire suspected she was thinking of him.

"How are you getting along over at Bellingham?" Mrs. Montgomery asked as they walked the short distance from the office to the ranch house.

"Did Seth tell you about the eggs hatching?"

"Oh, yes." Mrs. Montgomery hesitated, then continued. "He . . . didn't seem as happy as I might have expected him to be." She looked at Claire with a question in her eyes.

"He was probably exhausted. We were in the barn all night and one of the chicks had some trouble."

"I see."

But it was said in a way that indicated Mrs. Montgomery wasn't attributing Seth's lack of enthusiasm to his exhaustion and had hoped Claire would offer a different explanation.

But Claire was searching for explanations of her own.

They entered the ranch house and she eagerly looked around.

Although it was only one story, the ceilings were high, giving the illusion of vast space. The whole floor plan was laid out like a Spanish mission—a square with a central courtyard. Through the glass walls of the main living area, Claire could see a swimming pool and patio.

Unprepossessing on the outside, magnificent on the inside, Seth's home was a showplace.

"Do you like this ramble of a house?" Mrs. Montgomery asked after Claire had stared around her for an embarrassingly long time.

"It's beautiful. It wasn't at all what I expected."

"And what did you expect?"

"Oh, dirt floors, cow skulls, a big fireplace where you cooked . . . that sort of thing."

Seth's mother laughed. Her voice was definitely in the alto range, telling Claire where Seth had inherited his own deep voice. "No cow skulls here." She frowned. "But unfortunately, Seth's father did insist on mounting his deer heads in the den."

They shared a laugh and Mrs. Montgomery offered Claire some iced tea.

Walking to the kitchen, Mrs. Montgomery pointed out where different wings had been built onto the original house. "Seth's great-grandfather settled here with his own sketches for this house. They were crude, naturally, but it was clear that the mission plan was what he had in mind. My husband and I built the last part just after Seth was born."

She was silent a moment as she filled glasses with tea. "We'd planned to have a big family, but the Lord saw fit to bless us with quality and not quantity. Seth is a wonderful son."

Claire didn't know what to say. An apology didn't seem called for. "I don't have any brothers or sisters, either."

"So you and Seth have that in common." *And that's about the only thing*, she might have added, but didn't. "As the only son, he takes his family and ranching responsibilities quite seriously."

"So I've noticed."

Mrs. Montgomery smiled. "We've had a rough couple of years and he's determined that raising ostriches will bring prosperity to the area once again."

Claire let a giggle escape. "I heard part of that speech."

"Yes, he does go on about it."

They sat in a cheery nook off the kitchen. "This is my favorite part of the house," Mrs. Montgomery confided. "I sit here every morning and catch up on my paperwork and correspondence." She sipped her tea, then abruptly changed the subject. "Tell me, do you still plan to go to Paris when your year here is over?"

Claire's throat constricted, and she nearly choked. "If I possibly can." She told Seth's mother about receiving the letter from the academy.

"When did you get the news?"

"The letter was stuck in my screen door," Claire told her. "Seth was with me when I found it."

"The morning the eggs hatched?"

"Yes," Claire confirmed and Mrs. Montgomery nodded as though a missing puzzle piece had been found.

"No wonder Seth was so subdued."

"What do you mean?"

Mrs. Montgomery set down her glass and reached across the table to grip Claire's hand. "Can't you guess?"

Bewildered, Claire shook her head. "I won't leave before the year at Bellingham is up. I gave Seth my word."

"I know you wouldn't." With a sad smile, Mrs. Montgomery patted her hand and released it. "But you will leave eventually."

"Of course." Hadn't she always said so? "I'm not cut out for ranch life."

"Why, Seth tells me you've been a great help to him."

The soft expression in Mrs. Montgomery's eyes made Claire uncomfortable. "I've only been feeding the ostriches once a day, but even that's going to have to stop, now that I've got to work so hard on my designs. That's really what I wanted to discuss with Seth, but I haven't seen him lately."

Mrs. Montgomery gave her a look Claire couldn't interpret. "I have a feeling he'll be paying you a visit soon."

All the way back to Bellingham, Claire puzzled over her conversation with Seth's mother. The woman was trying to tell her something without coming right out and saying it, and Claire didn't have a clue.

She was surprised and pleased to see Seth's Jeep Cherokee parked in front of the ostrich barn when she arrived home.

Slamming the door of the truck, Claire sought him out and found him cleaning out the chicks' cage. "Boy, am I glad to see you," she said.

His smile was reserved, but it was still a smile.

"I was just looking for you over at your place."

"Oh? What for?"

Claire suppressed a sigh over their lost camaraderie. He was so obviously withdrawing emotionally and had been ever since she'd learned she was a finalist. The two must be connected, but she didn't know why. "We never discussed what to do about the chicks."

He sighed and brought his hands to his waist. "Yeah, the chicks are a pain and I think we've got another egg about to hatch, too. I talked to a breeder and he told me ninety percent of them hatch in the middle of the night."

"Oh, swell." Claire didn't need any more sleepless nights. "Seth, I want to talk with you."

"Good," he said, and twisted the top on a bottle of disinfectant. "I need to teach you how to care for the chicks."

Claire opened her mouth to protest, then stopped. What if there was an emergency? She'd need to know what to do. Might as well find out now.

"Cleaning up after them is the most important, especially when they're in the outside pen. The birds eat a lot of dirt and stones and you don't want them eating contaminated soil."

Claire's nose wrinkled.

"Somebody will have to look out for them at midday. Think you can handle that?" He glanced at her, a definite challenge in his eye.

"No," she answered. "Seth, I only have three weeks to get my entry ready for the judges and I haven't even begun sewing yet. In fact, I need to go to New York for fabric and notions." She'd just decided to this instant. She needed certain fabrics and she knew where she could get them in New York.

"I see," he said, unknowingly echoing his mother. He walked over to the hatcher, his back to Claire.

His attitude made her angry. "I don't think you see at all. I thought you'd be happy for me, but it's *so* obvious that you aren't. That hurts, Seth. I thought we were friends."

She heard a sigh and saw his shoulders slump. Then he turned to face her and she gasped at the raw pain in his eyes. "I thought we were more than friends," he said in his deep voice.

On some level, Claire must have known how he felt about her.

And on a deeper level, she knew he was right. They *were* more than friends.

Her eyes stung. She didn't want to be more than friends. She couldn't be more than friends.

She *wouldn't* be more than friends.

"Claire." When he said her name, Seth's face softened, and love shone from his eyes.

"No," she whispered and backed away, shaking her head. That's what his mother had been trying to tell her; Seth was in love with her.

"Claire, nothing has to change. I—"

"It's already changed! You don't want me to go to Paris!" She waited for him to deny it, not that she'd believe him, but he didn't.

"I guess I thought you wouldn't want to go to Paris."

There in the barn, amid the hum of the dehumidifier and the occasional peep of the chicks, Seth voiced her secret fear—that if she allowed herself to love him, she wouldn't want to go to Paris because it would take her away from him.

And she had to go to Paris. She had to.

She pressed her knuckles to her mouth, afraid she'd let the wrong words escape, afraid she'd tell him she loved him, too.

He must have seen it in her eyes, because he smiled, joy replacing the anguish. "Claire." He walked toward her and Claire panicked.

Whirling away, sobbing, she ran from the ostrich barn, away from the rancher who loved her.

CHAPTER ELEVEN

New York had lost its magic for Claire. She flew in on a Thursday and spent two days shopping. She stayed with Audrey, who was wildly enthusiastic about Claire's new designs.

"Ranch life agrees with you, darling," Audrey proclaimed. "These are fabulous. You won't forget me when you're famous, will you?"

"Of course not. You really like these?" They were in the back room of Audrey's shop, and Claire had spread out the four designs she'd chosen to submit to the academy. For daytime, she'd designed a wool suit and matching cape trimmed with ostrich feathers. For her resort wear, Claire had gone Western with a denim skirt and leather accents. Evening was, of course, her evening gown. She was using layers and layers of hand-painted chiffon in the exact colors of the twilight she'd been trying to capture. Across the bodice, she'd put Austrian crystals representing the stars.

"Claire, this is such a departure for you," Audrey marveled. "Elegant, yet distinctive. This is your best work."

"I know," Claire said quietly. It had taken the isolation of Bellingham for her to finally discover her own style.

"And this last one?" Audrey picked up the final sketch. "Is this quilting?"

Claire nodded. "Yes, I learned how to quilt, but I'm still a novice. Fortunately, I've been working on the material for a jacket."

"Will you have time to finish it?"

Shrugging, Claire said, "I'll have to, won't I?"

Back at Bellingham, Claire worked each day until she dropped into bed, and when she awoke, she went straight to her sewing machine.

But as hard as she worked, it wasn't enough to drive the memory of Seth's face out of her mind. Over and over she relived the moment when he'd told her he'd thought they were more than friends—and the moment she knew he was right.

It couldn't be, but she still missed him and missed talking with him and hearing him tell his stories about the ranch. He was as rooted to the Montgomery Rose as Claire was rootless. Family traditions were important to him. Claire's family had no traditions. She was barely aware of having a family at all. Her cousins and aunt hadn't communicated with her—not even through lawyers—since she'd moved to Bellingham more than two months ago.

She was exactly the wrong woman for Seth.

But still. At odd times, Claire found herself staring out the front window, hoping to see his truck. It was never there.

Once she went to the barn and was pleased to find three more chicks. A week later, there were ten altogether.

The contest deadline loomed ever closer. Tonight, her dressmaker's dummy was wearing the evening dress and Claire sat on the floor in front of it listening to the radio and pinning the hem. "Chiffon. I would have to pick yards and yards of chiffon, which will require a hand-rolled hem. Couldn't choose something I could sew by machine, oh, no.'' She picked up her scissors and trimmed a spot that sagged by the side seam. ''And a hand-quilted jacket, too.'' She'd had to abandon the intricate background work she'd originally planned, but the finished jacket would still be impressive.

She hoped.

She had eight days left of sewing each day until she was cross-eyed.

''A tropical storm watch is in effect for the Texas Gulf Coast from Freeport to Corpus Christi,'' the radio station informed her.

''At least I don't have to worry about that,'' Claire said, and pinned in the last pin.

Sighing, she stretched her arms and stood, hearing her knees creak. It was nearly eleven o'clock at night, and Claire debated whether to sleep now or start on the hem.

Pulling aside the curtains, she peered out her front window. A full moon illuminated the gravel yard and four feathered lumps.

And a black Jeep Cherokee.

Seth was probably in the barn. On impulse, Claire pushed open the door and walked down to see him.

It wasn't wise, but she couldn't stand not seeing him any longer, or the way they'd parted.

The lights were on in the hatchery, but no one was there.

''Seth?'' she called.

No answer.

Over in the hatcher, a lone ostrich chick lay wearily, half in and half out of his egg.

"Oh, you poor baby. Seth?"

Only a chorus of peeps from the older chicks answered her. "No, it's not time to eat, guys." Nevertheless, she tossed them a handful of chick feed from the helpfully labeled sack. The baby ostriches were so cute with their funny legs and stunted wings. Their brown and white feathers looked hairy, and their necks bore the dark speckled markings that would serve as camouflage in the wild. They were growing so fast.

Closing the feed sack, Claire glanced toward the barn door. Where was Seth? She decided she might as well clean the newly hatched chick off while she waited for him. After washing her hands in antibacterial soap, Claire prepared a warm bath for the chick and soaked him—or her—all by herself.

After putting the new baby in the warmer, Claire went outside to see if Seth's Jeep was still parked in the yard.

Yes, it was still there, gleaming in the moonlight. Something else was gleaming, as well. Stepping closer, Claire realized it was a cowboy hat.

And the cowboy was still under it. Seth had fallen asleep in his Jeep. The window was open, and with a sense of déjà vu, Claire reached in and shook his shoulder. As on that other night, he didn't respond.

Claire wasn't about to kiss him awake this time. "Seth!"

He groaned.

"The chick is fine. Come in and sleep on my couch."

"Claire?"

"The one and only."

Seth rubbed at his temple. "I fell asleep."

"I know. Come on inside."

Opening his eyes, he gazed at her. She could see him study her features as if reassuring himself that she still looked the same. "I was watching an egg."

"It hatched. Come inside," she repeated.

"No...I'll check on things out here and head on home."

"Don't be ridiculous. I don't want you falling asleep and crashing. How about some coffee?"

"Too late for coffee." He gave her a lopsided grin and sat up. "How about a glass of water?"

"I think I can manage that." She stepped back, and Seth climbed out of the Jeep.

"You can't keep up with the ostrich hatching all by yourself," Claire scolded him as they walked to the ranch house. "Why can't some of the other men spend their nights out here?"

"They've got their own ranches to run."

"So do you."

"Yeah, well." He sighed and opened the screen door for her. "I feel as though the ostriches are my responsibility. I was the one who talked everybody into investing in the birds. People are depending on me."

Taking advantage of him, more like. And the ranchers had been resentful of *her* because they thought she wasn't doing her share of work. Didn't they see what was happening now? Or hadn't Seth told them that Claire wasn't able to help out anymore? She suspected that might be the case. "You can be responsible without doing all the work by yourself."

"Other men take turns coming out in the morning."

"But what about the long nights?"

Shrugging, he said nothing.

"Seth, you can't continue at this pace—"

"Claire." He turned the full force of his gaze on her. "Money's tight. Nobody else can afford to pay the hands to come here and do the work. Just drop it, okay?"

Staring at the determined set of his jaw, Claire understood what Seth was doing. The other ranchers couldn't afford a true share of the work or costs involved in the ostrich venture, so Seth was taking up the slack. To save their pride, he didn't want anyone to know what he was doing.

What kind of woman wouldn't love a man like that?

What kind of woman wouldn't want to fling herself in his sheltering arms?

What kind of woman would turn down the possibility of love with this man?

Claire? Was Claire the kind of woman who could reject Seth?

How could the glittering lights of Paris outshine the steady glow of love in his eyes?

Shaken, she turned away and walked into the kitchen.

She had to be very careful. She'd known Seth just a couple of months. Paris had been a dream of hers for years. She wasn't ready to sacrifice it yet.

When a composed and newly resolved Claire returned with a huge glass of ice water, Seth was standing in front of her dressmaker's dummy. "Is this one of the designs you're sending off?"

She nodded. "It's supposed to look like dusk, you know, when the sky goes all purple and way up high you can see the stars?" She gestured to the strapless bodice. "The stars will be here. In fact—" she picked up a metal device that bore an uncanny resemblance to Seth's microchip gun "—I've got a gizmo here that'll put the stars on." She grinned.

He grinned back. "A gizmo, huh? How's it work?"

Picking up one of the shockingly expensive Austrian crystals she'd bought, Claire set it and a mount in the gun, positioned it and fired. "Behold, the evening star," she said.

"Do you ever wish on the evening star?" Seth asked her.

"Sometimes," she admitted.

"And do you ever get your wish?"

She couldn't meet his eyes. "Not yet."

He was silent for several seconds, then touched her cheek. "I want you to have your wish, Claire. So work hard and don't worry about the ostriches."

"I'm not worried about the ostriches," she couldn't help saying. "I'm worried about you."

He raised a hand as if to touch her, then let it fall. "I'll be fine."

"Get somebody to help you. I mean it, Seth."

"Okay."

But of course he didn't.

Claire tried not to be aware of the black vehicle that still appeared when a chick was ready to hatch. She also tried not to feel guilty about abandoning her evening chores, but didn't succeed. She wanted to be with Seth, and it was harder and harder to concentrate on her sewing.

"Tropical storm Daphne has been upgraded to a hurricane," cautioned the radio weatherman. "Stay tuned to this station for coordinates."

What coordinates? Claire wondered idly, and should she be writing them down? She was settling in for an evening of hemming and sewing on buttons. Flipping on the television and arranging herself on the couch, she caught the middle of yet another weather forecast. These Texans were obsessed with the weather.

And then she saw why.

On the weather map, the entire Gulf of Mexico was filled with a swirling pinwheel cloud. "As of now, landfall is projected for just north of Brownsville, Texas. Evacuation orders are in effect for low-lying areas." Claire could see that if the eye of that huge storm system passed over land, it made sense that the outer cloud fingers would be even further inland. Should she be concerned?

The movie Claire watched that evening was interrupted every half hour with storm updates and pictures of poor windblown reporters trying to stand upright on deserted beaches.

Hurricane Daphne was expected to make landfall sometime in the next two days. Claire had to ship her entry by the end of the week in order to make her deadline. What would happen to the mail service if planes couldn't fly?

Uneasily, she went to sleep that night, awaking to a gray sky.

She called Seth.

"Hurricanes don't usually affect us this far inland, but Daphne is a big storm." He sounded as tired as she was, and she ached for him. "If it stays offshore and picks up strength, then sometimes the eye plows inland before it breaks up and we get the rain and tornadoes. That's the real danger—all the tornadoes."

Claire listened closely, trying to hear any worry in his voice. He seemed more fatalistic than worried, and she wasn't reassured. "What about the ostriches?"

"They should be fine. The adults will hunker down, but the chicks need sheltering. As long as they're in the barn, they'll be okay."

What about me? Claire wanted to ask, but Seth didn't need any more to worry about.

He must have read her mind. "Do you know where your storm shelter is?" he asked.

"Sure," she lied, feeling like Dorothy in *The Wizard of Oz*.

"Then you're all set."

Right.

Immediately after hanging up, Claire went in search of the storm cellar. She found it, opened the plywood doors to a dank black pit and decided she'd rather be carried off by the storm than go down there.

Throughout the day, Claire sewed and sat glued to the television set as the winds picked up. In a way, it was exciting.

But in another way, it was distracting. Claire had two days left. She hated rushing all the last-minute details. The workmanship could make or break her entries. The day suit was complete except for the buttons, as was the denim outfit. She had more to do on the jacket quilting and, of course, miles of hem left on the evening gown.

The hurricane reports proved too disturbing, so Claire turned off the television and worked in silence, except for the gusts of moaning wind. She hemmed until she felt herself nodding to sleep, then grabbed the jeweling gun and applied stars. The more stars she put on, the more it looked like she'd need. Claire sighed. Would she ever finish?

Driving rains woke her up. She'd fallen asleep over the dress and put a crease in the chiffon. Shaking her head to clear it, Claire turned on the television and saw that the storm covered all of Texas, as if she couldn't figure it out for herself. The rain sounded as though the gravel in the yard was being thrown against the windows. Since it was too noisy to sleep, Claire decided she might as well work.

The hours passed, and Claire began to panic as she realized that she might not be able to finish in time. She certainly wasn't going to be able to stop working until the last button was sewn on. And when she did finish, how could she drive in this weather?

Hurricane Daphne had roared inland, sending waves of storm lines far into Texas and Louisiana.

It was so dark outside that Claire had to keep the lights on so she could see. She hoped the rain would let up in time for her to drive into Royerville and mail her package. Or should she trust the small Royerville post office? Maybe she should drive to Austin.

Or maybe she should charter a flight to Paris and deliver it herself.

As the hours wore on, Claire couldn't stop thinking about the ostriches. Seth would have called her if he needed her help, wouldn't he? If no one was available to feed the birds, surely he would have said something?

Claire caught herself listening for sounds of a truck. And she thought about Seth. And she thought about Seth checking on the ostriches. Finally, she couldn't stand it any longer. She needed to take a break anyway. The rain had slowed, so Claire ran through the mud and gravel to the ostrich barn.

She knew something was wrong as soon as she stepped inside.

Gray-green light streamed in from the gaping hole in the back of the converted horse stalls. The wind had ripped off an older section of wood, and water had poured in, soaking the chicks, exposing them to the wind and biting rain.

Only about half a dozen were still in the pens, and Claire had no idea how many were running loose outside. Those that were inside were wet, and a couple were ominously still.

She had to do something. They had to be dried off and protected from the wind and wet.

But her entry had to be mailed tomorrow, and she still had hemming and the buttons to sew and...

One of the chicks fell and didn't bother to get up. Alarmed, Claire knew they needed help and needed it now. She couldn't abandon them. She'd just have to hem faster.

Claire reached in and picked one of the smaller chicks out of the sandy mud. It was like hefting a Thanksgiving turkey out of the grocery freezer case.

Carrying the bird to the ranch house, Claire released it in the kitchen. She'd put them all in the kitchen until she could figure out what to do next.

The rains started up again, accompanied by boiling black clouds against a yellow-green sky. It was the ugliest sky Claire had ever seen.

One at a time, she carried three more birds to her kitchen, which was pretty well trashed by now. It would take her hours to clean the mess, but she'd have hours after she mailed off her entry.

The back of the barn bordered on Phoebe and Phineas's run, and Claire could see some chicks wandering in there. She supposed she ought to chase them down. Glancing at the sky, she ran into the house, retrieved some of her packing boxes and reassembled them. Tape. She needed tape.

The kitchen junk drawer had tape, and Claire gingerly pushed open the connecting door from the living room to the kitchen. She managed to get inside without any of the baby ostriches getting out, grabbed the tape and tried to back through the door. Unfortunately, an ostrich chick escaped. Claire chased him and pushed him in with his friends, but not before little ostrich footprints were tracked across her new rug.

Rain poured from the sinister sky as Claire dragged two huge boxes to the barn. She planned to corral the chicks in them temporarily.

Claire climbed through the hole in the side of the barn into the ostrich run just as a gust of wind shoved her back against the splintered wooden edge. And there she found her first runaway ostrich.

"Come here, baby," she crooned and set the quivering bird in a box.

Claire had no idea how long she chased terrified ostrich chicks under the disinterested gazes of Phineas and Phoebe, or even how many she should be looking for. She knew there were at least fifteen chicks altogether, maybe more.

She'd found eleven when she saw the funnel cloud. At first, since she was expecting the huge special-effects tornado from *The Wizard of Oz*, Claire didn't even realize what she was seeing. A black finger crooked out of the sky, disappeared and reappeared as a long snake, dangling toward earth. This was not a movie, this was real life.

"That's it. Everybody for himself," she hollered to the ostriches and abandoned her search.

Dragging the two boxes of chicks to the ranch house, she didn't bother going around to the kitchen, but brought them into the living room, mud and all.

Towels. She needed lots of towels. For her *and* the birds.

The wind howled and the sky suddenly darkened.

The lights dimmed, then flickered out, and a frightened Claire ran for the bathroom, expecting to encounter the Wicked Witch of the West any minute.

She sat in the dark on the tile floor, dripping, and waited.

And waited and shivered. And dripped some more.

Shouldn't there be noise? Didn't people say tornadoes sounded like freight trains?

She didn't hear a train, but she did hear a scratching. Cautiously, she reached above her head for the doorknob and opened the door.

And came face to beak with an ostrich chick.

"What are you doing here? Did you get scared?" Claire reached out her hands, feeling the need to cuddle something.

She'd just grasped the muddy bird to her when a thought occurred. "Where did you come from?" In answer, the bird pecked at her buttons.

The electricity was still off, so Claire set the chick down and groped her way out the door and down the hall.

Something fuzzy ran over her foot and she screamed. Tiny feet scrambled down the hallway, slipping on the wooden floor. Just then the gray light from the windows darkened as a human-shaped shadow loomed outside the door.

She screamed again.

"Claire!" Frantic pounding sounded on her front door. "Claire, answer me!"

"Seth!" Even from deep within the house, Claire recognized his voice and sagged in relief.

"Claire, are you okay?"

"I'm back here... Oh, no!" In the dim light, Claire could see that both boxes had collapsed into a pile of soggy cardboard, and the ostrich chicks had escaped.

"Claire! What's happening?"

Dodging chicks, Claire hurried to the front door, flung it open and was enveloped in a wet hug. Safe in Seth's arms, the terror of the last hour receded and Claire's knees threatened to give way.

"Are you all right?" Seth asked over and over, punctuating searching looks with frantic kisses.

Claire managed to nod. "Yes, but the ostriches escaped!" She pulled him through the door just as a chick raced across their path.

"What—"

"I checked on the birds and the storm had torn a hole in the barn. They were drowning, Seth."

"You went out in the storm to check on the ostriches?" He clutched her shoulders. "Oh, Claire, you could have been killed!" Anguish contorted his voice.

"But I couldn't let them die!" she protested. "And then I saw the tornado."

"I know." He hauled her close, and she felt the pounding of his heart. "I was out of my mind with worry," he murmured. "But it looks like the twister missed you."

With a relieved sigh, he pulled back and looked at her, his hair in dark clumps against his forehead. His hat was gone, and for the first time, she saw that a small cut bled above his left eye.

"You're hurt!" With gentle fingers, she explored the swelling.

"It's nothing." He waved off her concern. "Everybody's okay."

"The tornado hit the Montgomery Rose, didn't it?"

He nodded, his face grim.

"Bad?"

"The house is okay, but the office is a loss. The tornado skipped around."

Claire suspected things were much worse than Seth was letting on. "Then what are you doing here?"

He exhaled and blinked, as if relaxing for the first time in hours. "You're out here all alone and you wouldn't answer your telephone."

"I never heard it ring." He'd probably called when she was out playing tag with the ostriches.

"I thought something had happened to you and I couldn't stand it. Claire, if anything ever happened to you..."

He never finished because at that moment the lights flickered on and they both froze at the sight that greeted them.

Ostrich chicks and mud and droppings were everywhere. The rug was a disaster. And the chair...the sofa...

"My clothes!" Claire wailed and ran for her evening gown. "Get off!" She batted at two chicks that were pecking at the crystals in the bodice. "No," she breathed as she saw the extent of the damage. "Oh, no." It couldn't be. She squeezed her eyes shut, but when she opened them, the carnage remained.

The fragile chiffon was muddied and snagged. More than half the crystals had been pecked out, leaving dozens of jagged holes in the bodice.

"The dress is ruined," she whispered and raised her eyes to Seth. His jaw worked, but no words came out.

"It's ruined!" She shook the remnants of the dress at him, then wadded it up and threw it at a clump of ostrich chicks. They scattered, revealing the cream wool day suit, which was now decorated with a brown pattern of mud and something else Claire didn't want to think about.

The denim ensemble had met a similar fate. Only the quilted jacket had escaped, because it was hanging on the dressmaker's dummy.

"They've ruined everything!" Her voice rose in a wail as she absorbed the full extent of her loss.

Wordlessly, Seth wrapped his arms around her, but Claire didn't want to be held.

She beat against his chest. "My chance at Paris is ruined! My house is ruined!" She broke down and sobbed, burying her face against the same chest she'd just pounded. "My life is ruined, and all because of these stupid ostriches! I'm never going to get away from this horrible ranch!"

Seth just held her as she sobbed and the ostrich chicks ran amok. "I'm sorry about your contest," he said finally. "I'll send you to Paris. Tomorrow, if you like."

"No." She drew a shuddering breath. "I don't want to visit, I want to live there and study."

"That's what I'm offering, Claire." His voice was quiet yet determined.

Paris. He was offering her Paris.

Claire pulled back in openmouthed astonishment. Her dream was still alive. All she had to do was say yes, and she could be in Paris within days. She could take the ruined clothes and explain what happened. She wouldn't have a scholarship to study, but...

But she couldn't accept. It would mean Seth and the ranchers would lose everything.

Her smile turned wistful. "You forgot about my grandfather's will."

"I didn't forget."

"But the ranch...I wouldn't inherit it. And what about the ostriches?"

He sighed heavily and traced her cheek with his fingers. "The ostriches aren't important. You are."

The ostriches weren't important? Seth was a terrible liar. "If they're not important, what was I doing spending hours chasing them in the rain?"

The corners of his mouth turned up. "I don't know, Claire, why *did* you save them?"

Claire looked around her at the mess. "Good question."

Leaving Seth's arms, she bent and picked up the wadded chiffon evening dress. It was gorgeous, but ambitious, especially for the amount of time she had to sew it. Even if her finalist notification had arrived earlier, the quilted jacket alone would have taken the entire month allotted to her. And she hadn't just designed a simple, elegant day suit, no, she'd added a sweeping cape to make it that much harder. And the appliquéed leather on the denim outfit, what had she been thinking? She was too good a seamstress not to know her limits and how long it would take to fabricate the garments.

It was as though she'd deliberately set herself up for failure.

And when it looked as though she might achieve the impossible, she'd spent precious hours gathering the ostrich chicks instead of calling Seth for help.

She'd acted like a person who didn't want to go to Paris at all. In fact, hadn't Seth just offered to send her? And hadn't she turned him down?

Staring at the chiffon wreck in her hands, Claire grumbled, "I don't know why I bothered. The stupid birds will probably die from eating those crystals, anyway."

Seth smothered a laugh. "Not from something that small. And, uh, we could probably recover most of the stones if we keep the birds penned up."

"No, thanks," Claire said emphatically.

Seth chuckled softly. "So how about Paris?"

Claire looked from the dress in her hands to his dear face and realized what her heart had been trying to tell her. "Not without you." She crumpled the dress and tossed it over her shoulder.

He blinked. "Why?"

"Because I love you," she said, admitting what she'd tried to ignore for days. "And I don't want to go to Paris, or anywhere else, and live without you." A feeling of peace spread through her.

"But Claire..." Hope and torment crossed Seth's face. "I can't go to Paris with you. Not now and not for a long while."

"I know," she said lightly, and walked up to him. "So I don't want to go anymore." Standing on tiptoe and linking her arms around his neck, she added, "I want to stay here with you."

He gazed at her intently, his arms rigid at his sides. "Don't say something you'll regret. The situation looks bad now, but at the end of your year—" He broke off, his face pale.

Claire finished for him. "At the end of my year, you and the ranchers still won't be able to afford to buy my ranch, isn't that right?"

She knew it was, and so did Seth.

Still, he squared his shoulders. "We agreed—"

"Seth. With all the damage today and all you and the others have already invested, you won't have money to spare, will you?"

"I'll find it."

And Claire knew he would, too, even if it meant losing his own ranch. "You don't have to."

"Yes, I do," he countered with determination. "I gave you my word."

Shaking her head, Claire explained, "I want to be a successful designer and I thought going to Paris would help me become a success. I was so focused on getting to Paris, I lost track of the reason I wanted to go there in the first place."

"Claire, honey—"

He was only going to raise silly objections, so Claire continued talking. "I was searching for a direction I'd never been able to find in New York. But you know what? It took coming here and living in the quiet for me to finally develop my own style. I've done my best work here at Bellingham. Audrey's gone wild over the quilted jackets, and I've got so much more to learn. Quilting is a dying art and I—"

"But you don't like living here," he interrupted gently.

"Not all alone, no." She gazed at him through her lashes. "There isn't anything in my grandfather's will about me living here alone, is there?"

Shaking his head, Seth caressed her cheek with his knuckles. "You're talking a good game, but I know how important your career is to you. I could never ask you to give it up."

"I have no intention of giving up my designing," she stated firmly. "Frankly, a life of endless ranch chores doesn't appeal to me at all." Claire grimaced as an ostrich chick trotted past.

Seth exhaled and grinned. "That's my Claire. I was beginning to think the storm had addled your brains."

"No, it just let me see things clearly."

"It's about time." Seth captured her mouth in a searing kiss.

"I've loved you from the moment you stepped on the gravel in those ridiculous boots," he murmured several satisfying minutes later. "But I didn't think we had a chance."

Resting her head against him, Claire chuckled. "Neither did I."

Seth tilted her chin until he could gaze fully into her eyes. "I don't want you to have any regrets, because once you agree to stay here, I'm not going to let you go."

Claire felt a thrill at the resolve in his voice. "No regrets. I don't need Paris, but I do need you." She smiled. "So I want to stay here. But—" she nestled closer "—I don't want to stay alone."

"Claire." Seth crushed her lips to his. "I love you so much. Just try and keep me away."

* * *

Ten months later...

"If you'll sign here, Mrs. Montgomery, that will complete the final ownership transfer of your grandfather's ranch."

Claire signed and returned the pen to the lawyer. Bellingham belonged to her at last—and to her husband.

"Thanks, Aaron." Seth reached across the desk and shook the man's hand. "Glad things are finally settled."

Everyone stood. "I appreciate you folks abiding by the terms of the will the way you did. I don't think Beau intended for his granddaughter and her husband to have to live there, but he didn't figure on you two getting married."

"I don't know about that," Claire said, smiling. "His letters were full of his neighbor's praises. I just didn't realize he was talking about Seth at the time."

They all laughed and moved toward the door. "I'll have copies of the papers sent out to you," Aaron said. "Should I send them to Bellingham or to the Montgomery Rose?"

"The Rose," Seth told him, and slipped an arm around Claire's waist. "We'll be moving right after we get back from our honeymoon in Paris. My wife is going there for the spring fashion shows."

Tears of happiness misted Claire's eyes. Seth had been unmoving on this point. He was taking Claire to Paris, whether or not she wanted to go. Which, of course, she did.

"*My* wife has bought enough of your clothes to finance the trip, I'll bet," grumbled Aaron to Claire.

Swiping at the corner of her eye, Claire laughed. "Mrs. Hawthorne just has exquisite taste." And luckily for Claire, friends with similar taste. Her quilted jackets had become all the rage among Austin socialites.

"Actually," Seth informed him, "the ostrich pair I sold you is paying for the trip."

Aaron looked chagrined. "Yeah, I missed getting in on the ground floor of that deal. But who'd have thought it would turn profitable so fast?"

"Seth did," Claire said with a proud look at her husband.

"But I couldn't have done it alone," he replied, turning and kissing her lightly.

Aaron groaned. "Go on, get out of here. Shoo!" The lawyer hustled them out of his office. "Have fun in Paris."

"You've waited a long time for Paris," Seth said, as they walked toward the elevator.

"That's right, I have!" Claire agreed emphatically. "Just so you could go with me. And you, sir, had better make sure you were worth the wait!"

Seth raised an eyebrow and sent her a sizzling look. "Is there a doubt?"

Claire thought back over the past year's struggles and triumphs and smiled. "No. None at all."

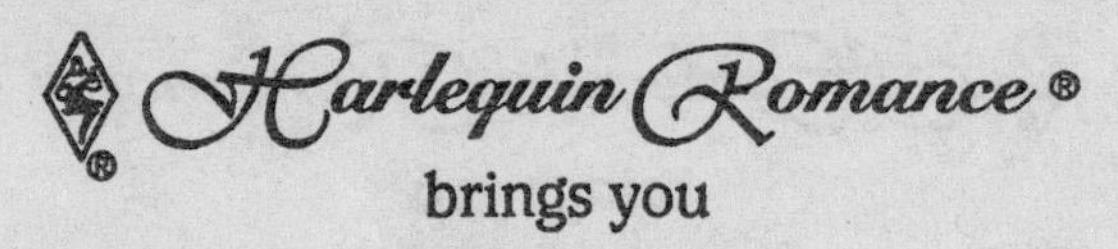

brings you

How the West was Wooed!

We've rounded up twelve of our most popular authors, and the result is a whole year of romance, Western style. Every month we'll be bringing you a spirited, independent woman whose heart is about to be lassoed by a rugged, handsome, one-hundred-percent cowboy! Watch for...

- September: #3426 *SOMETHING OLD, SOMETHING NEW*—
  Catherine Leigh
- October: #3428 *WYOMING WEDDING*—
  Barbara McMahon
- November: #3432 *THE COWBOY WANTS A WIFE*—
  Susan Fox
- December: #3437 *A CHRISTMAS WEDDING*—
  Jeanne Allan

Available wherever Harlequin books are sold.

Look us up on-line at: http://www.romance.net

HITCH-8

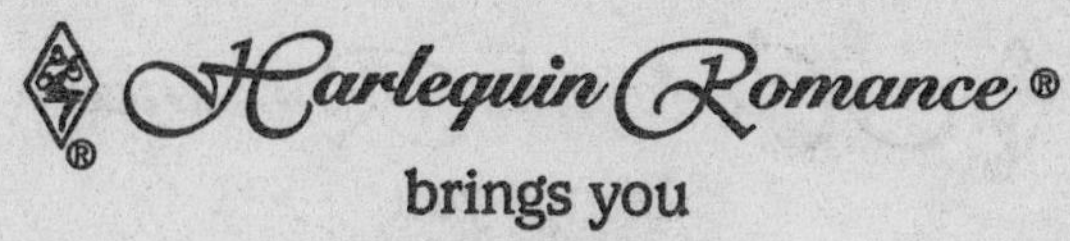

brings you

Some men are worth waiting for!

Every month for a whole year Harlequin Romance will be bringing you some of the world's most eligible men in our special **Holding Out for a Hero** miniseries. They're handsome, they're charming but, best of all, they're single! Twelve lucky women are about to discover that finding Mr. Right is not a problem—it's holding on to him!

In September watch for:

#3425 *REBEL IN DISGUISE*
by Lucy Gordon

Available wherever Harlequin books are sold.

Look us up on-line at: http://www.romance.net

HOFH-9

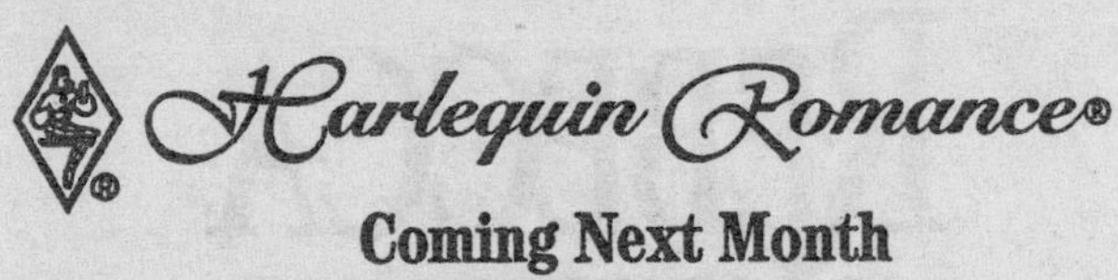

Coming Next Month

#3423 MARRYING THE BOSS! Leigh Michaels

All Keir Saunders was interested in was making money, and so when he needed a wife to complete a business deal, it seemed easiest to buy one! His secretary, Jessica, was the logical candidate. And though she was certain matrimony wasn't in her job description—how could she refuse a man like Keir?

#3424 A SIMPLE TEXAS WEDDING Ruth Jean Dale

It began simply enough when Trace Morgan hired Hope to organize his sister's engagement party.... But Trace didn't want the wedding to go ahead. And he certainly didn't want to fall in love with the hired help!

#3425 REBEL IN DISGUISE Lucy Gordon
Holding Out for a Hero

Jane was a cool, calm and collected bank manager. Gil Wakeham was a rebel. But Jane had accepted his offer of adventure—a summer spent with Gil and his adorable basset hound, Perry. The dog had stolen her sandwiches. Was Gil about to steal her heart?

#3426 SOMETHING OLD, SOMETHING NEW Catherine Leigh
Hitched!

Lily Alexander's husband, Saige, had been missing—presumed dead—for seven long years when he walked back into her life! And though Lily was overjoyed to see him, the timing was awkward, to say the least. Lily's wedding to her new fiancé was imminent! But Lily could hardly marry placid lawyer Randall when her sexy rancher husband refused to let her go!

AVAILABLE THIS MONTH:

#3419 KIT AND THE COWBOY
Rebecca Winters

#3420 EARTHBOUND ANGEL
Catherine George

#3421 TEMPORARY TEXAN
Heather Allison

#3422 DESPERATELY SEEKING ANNIE
Patricia Knoll

REBECCA

43 LIGHT STREET

YORK

FACE TO FACE

Bestselling author Rebecca York returns to "43 Light Street" for an original story of past secrets, deadly deceptions—and the most intimate betrayal.

She woke in a hospital—with amnesia...and with child. According to her rescuer, whose striking face is the last image she remembers, she's Justine Hollingsworth. But nothing about her life seems to fit, except for the baby inside her and Mike Lancer's arms around her. Consumed by forbidden passion and racked by nameless fear, she must discover if she is Justine...or the victim of some mind game. Her life—and her unborn child's—depends on it....

Don't miss ***Face To Face***—Available in October, wherever Harlequin books are sold.

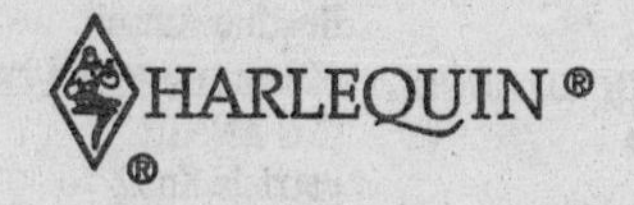

43FTF

Look us up on-line at: http://www.romance.net